Not Happily married

in Hollywood

Leonie Gant

ISBN-13: 978-0-9942990-5-5

Dedication

To my family.
I swear, none of the characters are based on any of you,
although I was tempted.

Chapter One

"Must say, I'm enjoying the view." The voice came from behind me as I was reaching over the desk to grab some paperwork. I wanted to smack my head against the desk. I'd let my guard down. Stupid rookie mistake. I straightened and turned around to find the husband of my latest client standing right behind me, showing a complete lack of awareness about personal space.

"Mr Wesson," I said through gritted teeth. "Could you please step back."

"Do you really want me to do that?" he asked silkily as he stroked a finger down the side of my face.

"Damn right I do," I said, the irritation evident in my voice.

His eyes flashed as if he wasn't used to being thwarted. He wasn't. I knew this. Especially by his wife's personal assistant. Unfortunately for him, I'm not just any PA. I work for Monique Petit. She has a stable of staff who work for the most difficult of clients and I have a reputation for working the worst of jobs.

My last job involved me taking a bullet to save my client's life. A move I questioned every day during the six weeks it took to heal from that particular assignment. During the media frenzy that followed, my client tearfully praised me as the best personal assistant she'd ever had, and a friend for life. She then quietly fired me and rehired her sister who had held the job before me. I had taken a bullet for her. Her sister had done a video on YouTube outlining her many, many flaws, yet she was the one who had the job. Of course, Monique ensured that I got a healthy severance bonus out it. If I was perfectly honest about it, I wasn't really all that sorry to see the end of that particular assignment.

I was hoping to settle into something a little more sedate. Instead I ended up with Adele Wesson, one of my favorite authors. I was so excited to get this job. Then I started and I discovered why she needed one of Monique's people. Her new husband, Eric Wesson, was younger than his glamorous wife and had, to put it mildly, a wandering eye. The man was completely amoral and was willing to put the moves on his wife's PA while his wife was in the room. Eric was quite simply sex personified. It went without saying he was good looking. His body was perfectly proportioned. Broad shoulders, slim hips, the body of a swimmer and I'd seen him in a pool. He was close to perfection. His golden hair always sat perfectly and his bright blues eyes honed in on a woman and made her feel that she was the center of the universe. I don't know if he exuded some kind of pheromone, but the second he walked into any room, women just started to fall at his feet, and he was definitely not a man to waste the opportunity.

Every single PA Adele had employed had fallen into his bed within a week. I'd started working for Adele two weeks ago and so far had managed to resist. I'd been given forewarning regarding what I would be facing. It helped that the criteria Monique had given me for the job included the terms prudish, uptight and less likely to give it up than a nun cloistered in a convent. I didn't know whether to be flattered or insulted by the fact she felt I met that criteria. Monique was very much aware that I was still furious at a certain homicide detective who was too chicken to face my mother. That probably helped her decide that I was perfect for the job. After I got shot protecting my last client, I woke up in the hospital to the face of Detective Jake Griffin, or Detective Hottie as my friends called him. We ended up sharing a toe curling kiss, celebrating my alive status, when my mother walked in on us and scared the big bad LAPD detective away.

Admittedly, she had just flown almost twenty-four hours from the other side of the world after being informed that her daughter had been shot. She had also, unfortunately, just been told the story about how Griffin had used an accidental assault charge to blackmail me into helping him investigate a murder, by threatening my Australian backside with deportation. The friend who had picked her up was my lawyer and Monique's husband. He may have also waxed lyrical about how the reason her baby was unconscious in a hospital bed with a bullet wound was Detective Griffin's fault. So when my jet lagged, ticked off, panicking with worry, Mama Bear of a mother walked into my hospital room and found said Detective with his tongue down my throat, she didn't react well. Needless to say, Griffin made himself scarce, and in the two months since, I hadn't heard a peep out of him. I've got to say, I'm not really happy, and at this stage I don't care to see him ever again. As far as I'm concerned, all men are jerks and had better stay out of my way. According to Monique that attitude put me in the perfect frame of mind for this job.

My mother stayed to help me, and probably herself, heal from the trauma of being shot. Two weeks ago I decided I couldn't take much more of her special brand of maternal love and begged Monique for a job. This was the one she threw my way, thinking it would prove if I was serious about coming back to work. In the end I decided it was a job and I would get to work with Adele Wesson. Definitely worth it. Nineteen sexual harassment incidents later I was beginning to question exactly how much I wanted this job. It wasn't as if the guy was dangerous or even creepy. He was simply persistent and could not understand how I was resisting him. I could understand though. Men sucked.

"Mr Wesson," I said.

"Please call me Eric," he said, leaning in again, smiling in that melting way he had.

Using the book I was carrying, I pressed it into his

3

admittedly rock hard chest and gave a slight shove.

"Mr Wesson, I am not now, nor will I ever be interested," I stated as firmly as I could, deciding that at that moment channeling my Grandma Rita might be the way to go. "What you are doing is disrespectful to not only your wife, but also to me. Please accept the fact that I am saying no for now and I am saying no forever."

His face crumpled and he looked like he was about to cry. No way was I falling for that again. The man was not above using every weapon in his arsenal, even tears to get his way. I learned that the second day, and had needed to employ a well-placed stomp of my heel on his foot to extricate myself that time.

Fortunately for me, showing her usual exquisite sense of timing, his wife walked in. Adele Wesson was a gifted author whose books had been translated into award winning movies. Of course with that much talent she had also been the scriptwriter. In her late forties, she had lost her adored first husband only a couple of years ago. Her marrying Eric Wesson had surprised many, but as I had found out, she was a vibrant woman, and Eric was Eric. Adele swept into the room. With her ash blonde hair and perfect pixie face, she looked like she could grace a magazine cover. Her bohemian look meant she always wore loose tops and skirts with scarves tying back her hair. She stopped her entrance and looked tiredly at Eric as he had me pressed up against the desk.

"Eric, please tell me you're not bothering Trudie again."

Rather than looking ashamed and stepping back as any normal person would, Eric tugged on a piece of my hair that had come loose from my ponytail.

"We were just being friendly," he said, looking his wife in the eye.

Pulling my hair out of his fingers and tucking it behind my ear, I clenched my jaw.

"If that is all, Ms Wesson, I'll leave you for today."

"Thank you, Trudie," she said as I walked past her. "I am truly sorry."

I knew she was. I did not understand her in the slightest. She didn't seem to mind what her husband did as long as it didn't interfere with her work. I couldn't do it, but my mom always said I had problems sharing. As I closed the door I heard the arguing start. It always happened like that. Ten minutes later though they'd be having sex. In the two weeks I'd been working in this house I had learned that relationships are weird and maybe it was better that I wasn't in one anymore. After having my heart ripped apart by my ex-fiancé a couple of years ago I'd only been tempted once and he got scared off by my mother.

Opening the door to my apartment I kicked off my shoes. Finding Mom's leftovers in the fridge I threw it into the microwave to heat it up. Mom was in bed so I ended up writing my report for the day including the three additional incidents with Eric Wesson. I contemplated admitting that this assignment was too much for me.

I moved around, my side still sometimes twinging from where I was shot. Thanks to Monique's quick thinking and decidedly skewed sense of priorities, a plastic surgeon had been called immediately after I got shot to fix the mess the bullet wound had made to my side. Luckily for my internal organs the bullet had been deflected by my rib. It had been cracked and the bullet had come out again about a couple of inches from the entry site. This had made a mess and Monique, assuming I would be wanting to be bikini ready for summer, had organized a friend of hers who was a top ranking plastic surgeon to fix it up. All this was done while I was unconscious or I would have informed Monique that no matter how good the surgeon was, I was not going to be bikini ready for summer.

I usually work with celebrities, actors, actresses, musicians or, as in Adele's case, authors. One of my strength's as a PA is that I blend into the background. I am completely average. I tie my slightly longer than shoulder length brown hair back into a pony tail and wear sensible shoes, pants and a simple top. My gray eyes are even unremarkable and they seem to change color depending on the clothes I'm wearing, making me a bit of a chameleon. I enjoy my food too much to have the perfect figure, so I'll go swimming but I'm a bit too self-conscious to wear that bikini, especially in LA.

Usually the men around my clients are far more interested in the bounty they have around them to even look twice at me. It doesn't bother me, it is simply a reality. As this assignment with Adele Wesson was proving, sometimes attention can be a bad thing. I wasn't fooling myself believing Eric Wesson was actually interested in me. The man was playing some kind of sick game with his wife and I was caught in the middle. That being said, I had noticed that he had upped the campaign in the last couple of days. My holding out must be becoming frustrating for him. Maybe I would need to speak to Monique about it.

Chapter Two

The next morning I let myself into Adele's house. Usually I would find Adele outside with her muse as she would call it. Adele credited the nature around her as the inspiration for her work. She had been hit by a stream of inspiration in her latest project. Almost every morning for the last two weeks I had found her outside. Looking through the house I could not find any sign of her or Eric. The cars were in the garage so I knew they had to be home. Heading towards Adele's bedroom, I knocked quietly on the door.

"Ms Wesson," I called out as I tried the doorknob. I slowly opened the door calling out again in case she didn't hear me. The room was empty, but the bed looked as if it hadn't been slept in which was very unusual. Dropping my head I contemplated my next move. The only room I hadn't checked was Eric Wesson's bedroom. The couple slept in separate bedrooms, something I found incomprehensible, but hey, it wasn't my marriage. I tried calling her cell only to hear it ringing on the bedside table. Adele never went anywhere without her cell. Reluctantly walking to Eric's room I knocked quietly on the door.

"Ms Wesson, are you in there?"

When there was no answer I knocked again, a little louder. I put my ear up against the door, trying desperately to hear something to indicate that I did not need to open it. There was complete silence.

"Ms Wesson," I called out loudly. "I am coming in now, I am concerned for you." I cringed. That didn't sound strange at all, but I really did not want to enter this room.

When the door was opened I saw the bed and strangled back the scream that rose in my throat. There, lying on the white sheets was Eric Wesson, blood covering the pillow underneath his head. Next to him lay Adele Wesson. I couldn't see any blood around her. If it wasn't for the blood, the two of them would look like they were just sleeping peacefully together. I crept towards the bed. I could see Adele's chest rising and I put my hand on her shoulder.

"Adele, wake up." I shook her gently but she didn't open her eyes. Raising my voice I yelled louder and shook harder. "Adele, wake up." No response.

I grabbed my cell out of my pocket and called emergency. When it answered I rushed ahead giving the address.

"Please, I need someone here right now. I just got to work and my boss and her husband are in bed. There is blood everywhere. I think she may be alive but I don't know about him. There is so much blood."

"Are you in any danger?" the dispatcher asked.

"I have no idea," I said, belatedly looking around, realizing that I could have walked in on anything.

"Can you find a place that's safe?" she said.

"I don't want to leave her," I said softly. "I think she's still alive."

"I've got police and paramedics coming. Everything is going to be okay." The dispatcher's calm voice grated over my jangled nerves.

I heard a crashing noise from the front door.

"I think they're here," I said.

"That's good," she said. "Now whatever you do, follow the police officer's directions. If they don't have to worry about you, then they can concentrate on your friend."

"Okay," I said and gulped as a cop stepped in the room and pointed a gun at me.

"Hands up," he yelled.

"I'm the one who called," I said as I put my hands above my head, holding up the cell phone. "I've got emergency on the line."

The cop took my phone and spoke to the dispatcher. Paramedics raced into the room and started working on Adele and Eric. The cop led me out of the house and sat me down on the front porch.

"What happened?" the cop asked.

"I don't know. I work here for Adele Wesson. I got to work about half an hour ago, same time as I always do and I found them like that. I left about seven last night and they were fine."

The cop nodded and started taking notes. A paramedic came over and put a blanket around my shoulders.

"Thank you," I said.

"Not a problem, not a pretty sight in there. I figured you're probably feeling a little shocky."

I looked up at him. "Is that a medical term?"

He grinned and I noticed he had a nice smile, kind and gentle with a small dimple in his chin.

"No, not really. It's before you actually go into shock, when you've seen something that you keep replaying in your mind."

I shivered. "Yes, well I think that qualifies. I don't think I'll be forgetting that scene in a hurry."

He put his hand into a pocket and pulled out a small chocolate bar. "Here have this, you'll feel better with a bit of sugar in you."

I looked at him carefully. "My mom's advice about strangers and candy is going through my head right about now."

He smiled again and his brown eyes lit up. He put out his hand. "Then we shouldn't be strangers anymore, my name is Ben."

I looked at him for a second and then grasped his hand. "I'm Trudie and now that you're no longer a stranger I'll take that candy bar."

Ben handed it over and I unwrapped it and popped it in my mouth.

"Feeling any better?" he asked.

"Yeah, I guess so."

I turned to the cop behind me.

"Any chance I can go to the hospital with Adele so she's not alone?"

"Afraid not. Homicide are going to need to speak to you."

"Eric didn't make it?" I asked softly.

"No he didn't," the cop said distractedly.

I bent my head, fighting back the tears. I didn't know why I was upset. I hadn't particularly liked the man. He had made my two weeks working for Adele difficult, but yesterday he had been alive and vital, and today he was dead. I felt an arm go around my shoulders and looked up at Ben's sympathetic face. I leaned my head against his chest and just let someone else be strong for a while. After a few minutes of leaning against Ben's warm chest and feeling his hand stroke my arm in sympathy I heard a throat being cleared. I pulled away from Ben and looked up, right into the face of the one man I had hoped I would not see.

The last time I had seen Detective Jake Griffin, his face had been worn and unshaven after sitting by my bedside for three days while I was unconscious after being shot. In the morning sunlight he looked great. His black hair was a bit longer than when I had seen him last. Those rebellious curls that grew at the ends were making a concerted effort to be more pronounced. His height and broad shoulders seemed to block everything else out of my line of sight. His green eyes though looked angry. In fact he looked really angry. His eyes were locked on the arm around my shoulder. He flicked out his badge.

"Detective Griffin, Homicide," he said to Ben. "We need to speak to the witness alone please."

Ben nodded but was slow to remove his arm and I could tell that it annoyed Griffin.

"You going to be okay?" he asked softly.

I shrugged as I pulled off the blanket and handed it to

him.

"Probably," I said. "Thanks for the chocolate."

He smiled. "Anytime, I'll just remember to stock up again for next time we meet."

I smiled back at him and watched him as he walked off. Knowing there was no way that I was going to put off the inevitable, I looked up into Ramos's impassive face and Griffin's scowling one.

"So are we doing this here or down at the station?" I asked.

"Station," Griffin growled, spinning around and walking off.

Getting up I directed my next question to Ramos. "What about my car? Can I drive it to the station so I have a way of getting home?"

Ramos didn't even have the grace to look apologetic. "You know the drill, crime scene techs need to look at it before we can release it."

"Great," I muttered.

Ramos touched me on the arm. "Sorry, Trudie, I really am."

Yeah, weren't we all.

Chapter Three

I was even more sorry when I was left to wait in the interrogation room for almost an hour. Griffin and Ramos had left me in there saying they just had to get a couple of things and would be a minute. An hour later, I was out of patience. Getting up from my chair I headed for the door, only to have it open as I was reaching for the doorknob. Griffin came through and my libido, which had taken a vacation while I was dealing with Eric Wesson, came roaring back.

"Going somewhere?" asked Griffin.

"Actually yes," I said while taking a step back from him. Not far, just far enough that I was out of temptation's reach. Despite the fact my head wanted nothing to do with Detective Griffin, my body was remembering that kiss, and was having a real hard time concentrating on anything other than the fact that his shirt was pulling tight across that chest. My lips felt dry and I swiped my tongue across them. Griffin seemed to zero in on the action and all of a sudden I started feeling very warm.

"I've got to go," I blurted out.

"You haven't answered our questions yet," Griffin said.

"Then maybe you should have started asking them about an hour ago," I said, the annoyance clear in my voice.

"Seems you haven't changed," Griffin said.

"What the hell do you mean by that?" I asked.

"Still can't do anything the easy way."

Okay, I'd just about had it. I sat down.

"I don't know what kind of game you are playing, keeping me sitting here for an hour, but we're not playing it anymore. You have ten minutes to ask any questions you want, and then I am walking. You can't hold me, so when the ten minutes are up, I am out of here and if you need to speak to me you can contact me through my attorney."

Griffin quirked his eyebrow. I'd forgotten how much that particular habit of his ticked me off.

"Very well, we'd better get started quickly hadn't we?" he said as he sat down. Ramos, who had followed him into the interrogation room took her seat beside him. "Tell us what happened this morning."

"I got to work at about eight, same as I always do. I let myself into the house. Usually there is noise happening at that time but I couldn't hear anything. I looked through the house to see if I could find Adele. I went to Eric's bedroom last, knocked on the door, and opened it, and found Eric and Adele in bed. Blood was on the pillow underneath Eric. I went up to the bed and saw that Adele was still breathing. I couldn't tell anything with Eric. I called 911 straight away and waited until police arrived."

"When was the last time that you saw them before this morning?" Griffin scribbled on his notepad.

"Last night about seven, just before I left."

"You have been working with Adele Wesson for two weeks, is that correct?"

"Yes it is." I wondered where he'd got that piece of information.

"Why did Adele Wesson hire one of Monique Petit's PAs? My understanding is you guys are used for difficult placements. Was Adele Wesson a problem client?" Griffin asked.

"Oh no," I said. "Adele is lovely, honestly one of the nicest clients I've ever had." Of course with my clients, we weren't really talking about the best examples of humanity, but still.

"Then why were you sent?" asked Ramos.

I really did not want to go into this.

"Is there a problem?" she asked.

I drew in a breath. "The problem is not Adele Wesson, it is her husband Eric. In the past he has made the working environment difficult for Adele's staff."

"Is he abusive?" asked Ramos.

I really did not want to go into this. I know Eric's behavior was not on me. That being said, I was embarrassed talking about it. Looking down at the table I continued.

"Eric Wesson has a habit of seducing Adele's staff, usually within the first few days of employment. Once he gets them into bed he ignores them and this can cause hurt feelings and at times, lawsuits."

"And you have been there two weeks," Griffin said and I could see that he was dying to ask the next question, but I was not giving him the answer.

"Yes, two weeks."

Griffin looked at Ramos. The annoyed look on her face was priceless.

"Did you have a sexual relationship with Eric Wesson?" she asked.

"No, I did not."

"You're saying that a man who seduced every one of his wife's employees never tried to seduce you." Griffin sounded almost disbelieving.

"No, I am not saying that," I said. "Over the last two weeks I have written up nineteen sexual harassment reports against Eric Wesson. Wait a minute, make that twenty-two. I did up a report last night for the three from yesterday."

"Twenty-two," Ramos said, sending a warning glance at Griffin. "What exactly was he doing?"

"It would depend on his mood and opportunity. He would try to corner me, brush up against me or talk to me suggestively. He flirted constantly."

"Why the hell did you stay?" Griffin asked, and I could see from the look on Ramos's face that she had wanted to ask that question.

"I don't do the easy jobs. I knew going in what the problem was, but Adele needed an assistant to get her through to finishing her latest novel. Eric Wesson was not dangerous. He was just persistent and he couldn't understand why I didn't get in bed with him. The man exuded sex appeal. I don't think anyone had ever said no to him before. He'd ramped it up a bit in the last few days but I was a challenge to him. If Monique had thought I would be in any danger I would not have been placed there. The reports I write are for Monique and they are just a record in case there is an issue that we haven't anticipated or planned for. Before placement Eric was informed that I had his number and he was not to try anything, but the guy was like a moth to a flame. Could not understand the word no."

"So you were willing to stay in a situation where you were sexually harassed on a daily basis." Griffin sounded incredulous and just a little bit judgmental.

That made me angry. "This kind of thing happens to women all the time. I could have walked away at any point. Most other women can't do that, especially not in this economy. If I walked away I would have possibly been replaced with someone else who couldn't cope with it. Adele's first assistant after marrying Eric was a nineteen year old who was absolutely devastated when she slept with him and he then tossed her out of the bed. Nothing the man did was illegal. I hate to speak badly of the dead but he was just a lousy human being. He never touched them first. It was a game of his that he would tempt them into touching him first."

"How were the two of them yesterday when you left?" Ramos asked.

"They were arguing." I shrugged. "They were always arguing."

"Do you know why?"

"Adele had just walked in to find Eric had cornered me against the desk in the study. I used the distraction of her entering the room to withdraw from the situation. She apologized to me for what had happened and when I closed the door I heard them start arguing about it. It always happened that way."

"What do you mean?" Ramos leaned forward.

"They had a strange relationship. Eric would sleep with anyone. I think Adele is still hung up on her first husband who died and doesn't really care about anything Eric did as long as it didn't impact on her work. They had separate bedrooms but they'd argue and then have sex. She once told me that despite his faults Eric was sublime in bed."

"Why would she tell you that?" Griffin asked, frowning.

"I don't know," I said, frustrated. "People tell me all kinds of things that they wouldn't talk about normally."

"Yes," said Ramos, "but if she's trying to keep you out of his bed why would she tell you he was so good? I would think that you would keep that information to yourself."

"Honestly," I said. "I don't think she cared if I slept with him, just as long as I kept working with her and didn't try to sue them."

"That's pretty messed up," said Ramos.

"Yes it is, but that's why I get paid the good money, because I deal with the messed up ones. Now I believe your ten minutes are up. Is my car ready to go?"

"Why the hurry? Did you manage to get a date at the murder scene this morning?" Griffin said as he leaned back in his chair, scowling at me. I was beginning to think my mom's warning was right. When you make faces like that all the time and the wind changes, they do become permanent.

Ramos jumped up. "Your car's all ready," she said brightly. "If you could just follow me."

As I left the station I looked back and saw Griffin leaning against the door frame, watching me thoughtfully.

Chapter Four

Thanks to Ramos I was soon heading towards my apartment, just in time to make sure that my mom was on her plane home to Australia. Don't get me wrong, I love my mom. She dropped everything to come to LA and nurse me back to health two months ago, and she hadn't wavered in looking after me. I love that about my mom. She is completely devoted to her kids and in the first few days after I got shot, I have to admit there's a part of me that enjoyed having her take care of me. That being said, two months later, I was kind of over it. What was, in the beginning, comforting, was beginning to smother and much as I loved the woman, I needed to get her on that plane today. Driving up to the apartment I saw my mom chatting merrily away to Miss Betsy, the owner and sometimes maintenance person of the complex that I live in. The two of them had bonded during my recovery period and I had a feeling that I would be having a serious conversation with Miss Betsy about what information could be shared with my mother during the weekly phone calls which I knew were now going to happen between the two women.

"Hi, Mom," I said as I got out of my car.

"Hi, honey, I was worried you were going to be late. Then I remembered how desperate you are to get rid of me."

"I wouldn't say desperate," I smiled at her. "Maybe just wildly enthusiastic."

My mom stuck her tongue out at me. Sometimes she seems to have the wisdom of the ages and at other times the woman acts like she is in kindergarten. Looking at her, you wouldn't pick her as my mother with her blonde hair, blue eyes, petite slim figure and bubbly personality. I am not overly tall but I feel like I dwarf the woman. With my brown hair, gray eyes and serious disposition, I am more my father's daughter. My younger sister Katie is like my mom. They are just people who walk into a room and ten minutes later have great friends who are planning on going away on holiday together. I am more likely to end up as agony aunt to some poor woman who's just found out that her husband is cheating on her. Not sure what it is about me but I must give out some sympathetic vibe that people decide to dump all their problems on. My brother Jamie ended up a combination of the best of my parents. Unfortunately, he was also a teenage boy so that wonderful personality was currently hidden underneath layers of hormones and angst, only occasionally making itself known. I still missed seeing him though. The only downside to working on the other side of the world. Not easy to pop in to see them when you are looking at a twenty-four hour flight.

"Are you ready to get going?" I asked brightly, realizing suddenly that the back of my eyes were prickling with heat. I shoved my sunglasses back on and went to grab her bags. No way could I let that woman know that I was about to start crying because I was going to miss my mommy. First sign of weakness and she would change her mind and I'd have her here for another month. I loved the woman but I needed a break.

Standing at the airport a couple of hours later, hugging my mother goodbye, I felt those tears come back.

"I love you, Mom. Thanks for everything you did for me."

My mom smiled that beautiful smile that she reserves for the moment when her children actually thank her for one of the many sacrifices she makes for them.

"You're my baby girl, I'd walk through fire for you," she said into my hair as she hugged me fiercely.

She started to walk away and then stopped and turned.

"I wasn't sure whether I should tell you this," she said,

"but you're a smart girl and you need to know."

She grabbed hold of my hand and squeezed tightly.

"A couple of days ago your father called. Paul went out to see him at the farm."

She searched my face intently looking for my reaction. All I was thinking was that I hoped he wore a full suit of armor. My dad hated my ex-fiancé with a passion he reserved for politicians and people who talked at the movies.

Obviously thinking that it was safe to go on, my mom continued.

"He said he made a mistake, he should never have let you go."

"He didn't let me go," I said. "He dumped me when I needed him most."

Look at that, the bitterness was still there.

"I know, sweetheart. I'm not saying that you should do anything. I'm giving you the information. Toss it aside if you want but he may try to contact you at some point. I thought it was only fair that you should be prepared."

Right there, that is my mom. She will try to protect you from anything that comes your way but if she knew there was something coming that she couldn't protect you from, she would give you every weapon in her arsenal to protect yourself.

I hugged her again. "I'm okay, Mom. Don't worry about me. Have a good flight and give Dad, Katie and Jamie all my love. Tell them I miss them so much."

"I will," she said, and I could see the tears glistening in her eyes. Well at least I wasn't the only one on the verge of crying. With that she walked away.

I got back in the car and headed home on autopilot, feeling numb. When I got to my apartment I couldn't make myself get out of the car so I stopped and rested my head on the steering wheel. How could Paul do that? I took in a shaky, deep breath. Since that day two years ago when Paul let me down, I have never looked back and I wasn't going to start today. I doubt Paul would even recognize me now. I was no longer anything like the girl he originally asked to marry him.

Chapter Five

I was startled by a sudden tapping on my window. Looking up, I saw the concerned face of one of my neighbors. Sean was a sixteen year old kid that I'd met a couple of months ago. His mother's boyfriend had tossed him out and he'd been living on the streets when I met him. Small and skinny for his age, he had a crazy mop of red hair. He reminded me of my little brother, Jamie, and I couldn't handle the thought of what could happen to him on the streets. Next thing I knew I'd ended up with him sleeping on my couch. After I got shot and my mom came to stay, I moved into one of the larger apartments with two bedrooms and Sean ended up staying in my old one bedroom apartment. The owner of the building, Miss Betsy, put Sean to work with maintenance to pay for his accommodation. We had also organized that he go back to school. Between Miss Betsy and me, we made sure that he was fed, did his homework and went to school. Between us we had become a family. Not the ideal situation but considering his other options included foster care or the streets, it was the best we could come up with.

"Are you okay?" he asked, a worried look in his eyes.

Unfortunately, a side effect of my getting shot was that Sean was now perpetually worried about me. I was constantly being asked how I felt, whether I needed anything, or if there was any way he could help me.

"I'm fine," I said with a smile. "Just missing my mom."

Sean looked skeptical. I wasn't surprised. I've been told that I am a shocking liar and Sean is a perceptive kid. Also when my mom found out about Sean's background, the poor boy had been subjected to her special brand of motherly love which could, on occasion, be smothering. I think he liked my mom but the day he found her ironing his underwear was one that I don't think he has yet recovered from.

As I opened my car door and got out I realized that Sean hadn't been alone when I pulled up.

"Trudie," Detective Griffin said as he walked over to us.

"Detective Griffin." I nodded back to him, crossing my arms.

Hey, I know it was a defensive move but I was stuck with it until he turned away.

"I need to do a walk through at the Wesson property and was hoping you would help me," he said.

"Why me?" I asked mutinously. "I've only been there two weeks, I wouldn't know the property well enough to tell you anything."

"Maybe, but you were there the night before. From the looks of it Eric was dead within hours of you being there."

I looked at him suspiciously.

"Please," he grumbled.

"See," I said graciously. "You only had to ask nicely, and I'm happy to help you."

"You don't even try to make things easy do you?" he asked.

"This is me making things easy," I said as we walked to his car. "If I was trying to be difficult there is no way I would be going anywhere with you."

The car was silent for a while as we drove.

"Is this Ramos's car?" I asked.

"No," said Griffin. "Why?"

"This car is surprisingly clean, I would not have picked it for a male cop's car," I said as I twisted around to see if there was a mess in the back seat.

"That is the conversation you want to have?" Griffin asked, looking a little put out as we pulled up to Adele Wesson's house.

"What do you mean?" I asked.

"Nothing at all," he said as he got out of the car.

Undoing the seatbelt and opening my own door, I looked at him. I swear, they say women are moody and unpredictable but one of these days somebody is going to work out that men are just as bad. I didn't have a clue most of the time. That being said, I was enjoying the view. The man seemed to have no communication skills whatsoever but following him to the house I could see that he still filled out a pair of jeans very nicely. All of a sudden Griffin stopped abruptly. Not having seen him stop, and being a bit distracted by the way those jeans were molded to his legs, I ran into his back and bounced off.

"What are you doing?" he asked.

I prayed that the warm sensation that I could feel was the late afternoon sun and not the blush of embarrassment that I knew was crawling up my face. I really hoped he wouldn't work out what I had been looking at. I peeked up and wanted to groan. From the smile starting to spread across his face, I could tell that he knew exactly where my eyes had been.

"I tripped," I mumbled.

"Uh huh," he said, that grin now spread wide.

"So what am I looking for?" I asked. I wanted to kick myself when I saw the way his eyebrow quirked up, and that knowing smile of his didn't lessen.

"The walk through," I clarified. "You asked me to help you with the walk through. What exactly is it that I am looking for?"

Griffin paused for a couple of seconds, just to torment me I'm sure of it, and then turned around.

"We need to go through and I want you to tell me if there is anything obviously out of place or catches your eye. I need you to think back to last night and see if there is anything different that will give us an idea of anyone else being in here. We can start with you taking me through what you did this morning when you arrived. Give me a good sense of what happened and what you saw."

Opening the front door, he waved me on ahead.

"Well then," I said. "When I walked in, the first thing that I noticed was the silence. This house is not a quiet one, usually there is music on or a television going in the background. This house is small compared to some that I've worked in so rooms don't feel isolated. Eric doesn't, I mean, he didn't seem to work. I think he called himself an entrepreneur but I never saw any evidence that he was actually working at anything. Usually when I got here in the morning the coffee machine was going and Adele would be awake. Sometimes she'd be doing yoga in the back yard or if she had been up a while she would have already started work. Adele was always an early riser."

"Did she have any trouble with sleeping?" Griffin asked.

"I think she did," I replied. "Sometimes when I got here you could see the dark rings under her eyes."

"You said Adele and Eric slept in different rooms, how bad were the problems in the marriage?" Griffin asked.

"The guy was a jerk," I said. "Adele was the sweetest, kindest person I knew. In my job I cop a lot of abuse and insanity from some of the clients but Adele was a dream to work for. I personally have no idea why she married Eric. From what I understand she adored her first husband. She'd talk about him sometimes and you could just see how much she loved him. I think when he died she was so wrapped in her grief and loss that she was easy pickings for Eric. Despite the fact she lives very simply the woman is very wealthy. She just doesn't care about the money. Eric, on the other hand, really cared about the money."

"Do you think she was capable of killing him to get rid of him?" Griffin asked.

"No," I answered quickly.

"You seem pretty sure of that," Griffin replied.

"I am, I cannot believe that she is capable of killing anyone," I said confidently.

"What about you?" Griffin asked.

I looked at him. "Me, you're going to ask me if I killed

him."

"The man was sexually harassing you in a job you loved. Jobs are scarce these days. You needed the money and you yourself said the marriage was a mess. You would be doing Adele Wesson a favor."

"Yes, because killing unwanted spouses is just another service I provide for my clients, along with diary scheduling and dry-cleaning runs," I said sarcastically.

"Okay, so if neither you nor Adele Wesson killed Eric." He peered at me and I returned the look with what I hoped was an expression that told him what I thought of that theory. "Then who else would want to?"

"Take your pick. Former staff members of Adele's, angry husbands, irate fathers, every woman he had ever come across. The man was physically incapable of keeping it in his pants. He was almost a caricature of the worst that women think of men. For the last two weeks he had hassled me constantly. I have never seen a man work so hard to get into the pants of a woman he had absolutely no interest in, outside of irritating his wife. It seemed the more that Adele liked having me working for her, the more effort he put into it. That being said, if he closed his eyes there is no way that he would be able to describe what I looked like."

"Do you often get that problem?" asked Griffin.

"What problem?" I replied.

"Sexually harassed at work."

"Like I said, Monique gets the difficult jobs and out of those difficult jobs you have the ones that border on painful. I have proved to Monique that I can handle those jobs. I find them challenging and I get paid very well for them. In answer to your question as to whether I was afraid of losing the job here, Monique has a waiting list of clients who she would be happy to pass me to. Last night I was actually considering quitting from this job because I was finding Eric's attention more insistent than I had anticipated. I assumed he would give up way before now but he was getting more persistent with each rejection."

"Thought of giving in?" he asked

"No, I can definitely say that I was not interested in giving in to him. The more I knew him, the less attractive he became. He was like a petulant child that wasn't getting what he wanted. Everything else being equal, he was definitely not my type."

"Really, so what is your type?" asked Griffin, leaning back against a wall.

"I'll know him when I see him," I said, definitely not wanting to get into this with him.

"Once I'd been through all the rooms and determined nobody was here, I went up to Adele's bedroom," I said, changing the subject hurriedly.

Griffin followed me towards the back of the house where the bedrooms were. Opening the door, I was relieved to see the room was relatively untouched by the police. Everything seemed to be in its place, exactly as it always was. The bed was immaculately made and at that I stopped.

"The bed looks wrong," I said.

"Why, what's wrong with it? Looks like it's fine to me."

"Yes, it looks perfect, that's what's wrong. I made this bed yesterday."

"You made the bed," Griffin said slowly.

"Yes, I made the bed. The housekeeper that Adele has doesn't live on the property, she comes in about the same time that I do. One of her jobs is making the bed. She didn't come in yesterday. One of her kids came down with chickenpox and had to stay home from school, so she called and we expected not to see her for a week. Adele is useless at all kinds of housework, especially at the moment when she's in the middle of writing. Inspiration hits and she forgets everything else. I even have to stop her to eat and take bathroom breaks. With the housekeeper not being here for a week, I helped out yesterday with those things that she would normally do, including making

Adele's bed. That is not the way I made Adele's bed. I am not that much of a perfectionist, I mean seriously, look at those corners," I marveled.

"They look fine to me," Griffin said, "That's how I do my corners."

"I am not critiquing the way the bed was made, I am saying I made it yesterday morning, but not like that. Between then and now someone else made the bed. Why would anyone do that?"

"Good question," said Griffin. "I don't think the crime scene techs did this room. Might be a good idea to get them back in here to have a look to see if they find something. Anything else look out of place?"

"Not that I can see," I said. "It all looks pretty much the same as it did yesterday when I was in here, other than the bed."

"I want you to have a look at Eric's bedroom now," Griffin said.

"No point," I said. "This morning was the first time I went into the bedroom, and that was just because I couldn't find Adele anywhere else in the house. My instincts were screaming at me that something was very wrong, I wouldn't have any idea what Eric's room was supposed to look like."

"Really, you've never been in that room?" Griffin asked.

"Nope, avoided it like the plague," I said cheerfully. "Considering the way Eric had been acting, that was one risk I was not willing to take."

"Did you see anything this morning that looked out of place?"

"Besides Adele actually having spent the night in his room, no."

"Okay," said Griffin. "Is there anything else that you wish to tell me about that could help with this investigation."

"You still think I'm keeping something from you?" I

asked.

"Not exactly," he said, at least having the good grace to look embarrassed. "Just sometimes things will come back to you at the strangest times. I need to know that you will give me that information."

"I don't deliberately set out to make your life difficult," I said.

"Yet you do it so well," Griffin said with just a touch of sarcasm.

Chapter Six

As Griffin drove me home I kept going over everything that I had seen during the day. I wasn't concentrating on the road and when he parked I looked around.

"This isn't my place," I said. "What are we doing here?"

"Having dinner," Griffin said.

"Having dinner," I repeated. "Like a date?"

"Sure, like a date," he said.

"According to my admittedly limited understanding of American courting culture, a date generally involves somebody being asked. I wasn't asked so I believe this may constitute a kidnapping, not a date."

Griffin looked at me sourly. "Look, it's late, I'm booked for dinner with my dad and I don't have time to take you home and then come back here," he said as he got out of the car.

"Well don't I just feel special," I grumbled as I followed him.

Standing at the door I almost choked when Griffin knocked.

"You're knocking at your father's door," I said, scandalized.

"It isn't my house, I'm not just going to walk in. Don't tell me, you would."

"I have keys to my parent's house. My grandparents once went out to get groceries and came back to find me fast asleep on their couch. They live five hours away from my parent's home, but I had a free day and wanted to see them."

"Wasn't the door locked?" Griffin asked.

"Farm in the middle of nowhere, people who grew up in a simpler time." I shrugged. "The door was never locked."

At that point the door opened.

"Hi, Dad," said Griffin. "This is Trudie. Trudie, this is my dad, Lee."

"You're early," the man at the door said and then turned around and walked back in the house.

"Early," I repeated. "You could have taken me home."

"I just wanted to prolong the joy of being in your company," Griffin said sarcastically.

"Careful," I said as I followed the older man into the house with Griffin trailing behind me. "I might just get the idea that you like me."

Dinner with the Griffin men was an experience that I was not used to. The table was completely silent during the meal, barely interrupted by mumbled requests for the salt. Eyre family meals had a habit of descending into the raucous and at times inappropriate conversation. My parents were strict believers in the fact that the meal was the only time most of the family came together. It was also the only time they had a captive audience in their children. Most of my life lessons throughout childhood had been discussed at the dinner table. I eyed the two of them carefully. Not being distracted by discussion the two men seemed intent on completing their meal as quietly and efficiently as possible. Determined not to be left behind I tackled my own, quite large, plate. The bowl of pasta was simple but delicious. My only issue was it was huge. Unfortunately I had been brought up by my parents to always finish what was on the plate when someone else had cooked for me. I know, really bad advice when it comes to weight control, but my parents were sticklers for being polite when in someone else's home.

Just as dinner was finishing Griffin's cell started ringing.

"Excuse me," he said as he left the room, leaving his father and me to uncomfortably eye each other over the table.

"Delicious meal," I ventured.

He stopped and looked at me shrewdly. I could see he was about to say something but Griffin came back into the room.

"I'm sorry but I have to go. Something has come up on a case I'm working and I have to follow it up now."

"Eric?" I asked curiously.

"No, another case," Griffin said abruptly. "Dad, can you take Trudie home for me?"

"Sure, son," Lee said.

Griffin looked at me as if undecided about what to do next.

"I'll see you later," he said, turned around and walked out of the house, leaving me with a man that I didn't know. I looked at Lee.

"Want a beer?" he asked, getting up to the refrigerator, grabbing one and opening it in one fluid move.

"No thank you," I said. "Look, I'll just grab a taxi and head home. Don't worry about a ride."

"No, no, I'll just finish the beer and then I'll drive you home."

"I'm sorry but I don't want to get into a car with you if you've had a beer," I said, cringing with embarrassment.

Lee stopped drinking and looked at me, dumbfounded.

I rushed on feeling like an idiot. "I'm not telling you what to do. I got hit by a drunk driver a couple of years ago and since then I have a problem with cars and I have an even bigger problem with alcohol and cars."

"I've only just started it."

"It doesn't matter, this is my issue we're talking about. Even a sip freaks me out. I know it's not rational and I'm sorry if you're offended but I think me getting a taxi is a better idea."

Lee went to turn up the bottle and pour it down the sink.

"No, don't do that. I'm not trying to tell you what to do. I'm just a little nutty when it comes to this issue."

I could feel the heat rising in my cheeks. I was usually so good at hiding my problems.

"Honey, just sit down," Lee said. "I'm going to pour out the rest of the beer. We are going to sit down and get to know each other, until you feel comfortable again, and then I will take you home."

"You don't have to," I protested.

"Geez, woman, you're stubborn. Just sit down for goodness sake."

I sat. "My mom calls it being strong willed," I said quietly.

"I'm sure she makes your dad's life interesting," Lee replied.

"He doesn't complain," I smiled. "But then my dad is a very smart man."

"So," said Lee as he settled himself into a well-worn chair. "My boy brings home a woman to meet his father. What I want to know is what are you doing with my son?"

"Just to clarify," I said. "You are starting this conversation by asking me what my intentions are towards your son, your fully grown police officer son."

Lee barked out a laugh and I could see the response was not a common one as it sounded a bit rusty. "I guess I am. Don't worry, this is as new to me as it is to you. Jake's never brought a woman home before, so I'm probably going from an old script on this one."

"Well," I said. "Since I have met Griffin he has hauled me to the station to be interrogated several times. He has threatened to deport me when I accidentally assaulted him. He bolted when he met my mother and I haven't seen him in two months. I meet up with him again today and he spends pretty much the entire day scowling at me, and then he kidnaps me and dumps me here. At this point I've got to say that if you are concerned for his virtue with me, don't worry, it is completely safe."

"That explains the weird mood he's been in lately," Lee muttered. "Look, I don't want to interfere with whatever it is that my boy's doing."

"But you're going to aren't you?"

"Only because I think he's going to screw this up and I've never seen him look at a woman like he looks at you."

I stared at Lee incredulously. "I don't know what you think you are seeing, but the expression that he has when he looks at me is generally anger, with some exasperation and a little bit of annoyance. Maybe there's a flash of attraction every now and then but that is it."

"Not exactly how I'm interpreting it, honey."

"So you're the expert on feelings in your family then?" I asked.

Once again a bark of laughter came from Lee. "No, that's the goddamn truth. Jake's mama was a rich college girl. She was beautiful, had the most amazing green eyes, only thing she gave Jake. We pretty much fell in lust straight away. She liked the whole big strong cop thing. She got pregnant, we got married. When Jake was a few months old I got home from work, she passed him to me, said she couldn't be a cop's wife anymore and walked out the door. Sometime later I got divorce papers and neither Jake nor I have seen her since. My parents were gone at that point so the only people to help me were the guys at the precinct. Jake's never really had a female influence in his life. Lucky for me, he didn't go off the rails when he was a teenager, but he's never been serious enough about a woman to bring her to dinner with me, until today." He looked at me meaningfully.

"I think you're reading too much into this. Me being here doesn't mean anything," I protested. "We were doing a walk through at a crime scene that I was a witness at. He just didn't have time to get me home before coming here."

"Of course," Lee replied.

"Kind of strong willed yourself aren't you?" I sighed.

He smiled at me.

"Look, I honestly don't know what it is your son wants from me."

Lee quirked an eyebrow up, looked like it was a family trait.

"Well of course I know," I said hurriedly, my cheeks heating up again. "I just haven't seen him in two months, he disappeared right after I thought there was something beginning between us."

"Jake doesn't do permanent," his father said. "Part of that's my fault. After the number his mom pulled on us, I just wasn't interested in trying it again. Jake saw this and learned from it, probably not in the best way. I was careful to never bring a woman home, didn't want him to get attached just to have them walk away. Jake grew up focused and strong. He wanted to be a cop just like his old man. He wanted to be a great cop, nothing was going to get in the way of that."

"Why are you telling me this?" I asked.

"Because I'm getting old and looking at my regrets in life. When I see him look at you I can see a future in his eyes that doesn't revolve around just being a cop. I want more for my boy than I had and you are the closest I've been to getting it."

"Look, I don't know what to say," I said carefully. "What is or isn't between us should stay like that. I can see that your son is a good man and I won't say that I'm not attracted to him, but if anything happens between us, it is between us. You can't push me and you definitely can't push him. Do you understand that?"

"Yes," Lee said grudgingly. "I just don't want him to screw it up. I think you would be good for him and Lord knows the boy is a dumbass sometimes when it comes to feelings and all that crap."

I put my hand on his arm. "The fact that you care this much makes you a good dad," I said. "Although for future reference, the next woman Griffin brings and dumps on you might not be so accepting of the whole intention's interrogation."

"Just never had to do it before so I'm not sure of what

the protocol is," he said.

"Me neither," I said. "But I'm pretty sure the next step is you telling me embarrassing stories about his childhood and showing me his naked baby pictures."

Chapter Seven

The ringing of the telephone was jarring and I grabbed it.

"Where the hell are you?"

"Dad?" I asked, confusion in my voice.

"No, it is not your father, although I'm sure he would have some questions for you. It's Jake," Griffin growled out.

"Oh, morning, what's up?" I sat up on the couch I had been lying on.

"Sean says he can't find you and your car is still parked outside your place." He was still growling. Did not seem to be a morning person.

"Why are you talking to Sean?" I really needed coffee. This conversation was not making any sense at all.

"Beside the point, Trudie. Back to the original question, where are you?"

"I'm still at your dad's house."

"Why on earth would you still be there?" He sounded amazed.

"We started talking and then it got late. I must have fallen asleep on the couch because that's where I am now, and it's actually quite comfortable, more than I thought it would be," I said as I pushed down on the cushions.

"My dad does not talk."

I looked up to see Lee holding out a coffee towards me.

"Oh that is so wrong, he is really the chatty Kathy when you get him going. He spent the night telling me everything about you, including that one time with the cheerleader… Oh here he is with my morning coffee, I'll talk to you later."

Turning off my cell, I wrapped my hands around the

steaming cup.

"Thank you," I said.

"Do you enjoy torturing my son?" Lee asked.

"Makes my morning that much brighter," I said, blowing across the top of the mug.

"I didn't say anything about Jake and a cheerleader," Lee said.

"I saw the football photo of him in high school on the mantle, trust me, somewhere there is a story with a cheerleader."

"I don't think my boy is prepared for you," Lee said chuckling. "I believe I'm going to enjoy this."

"Well you'd better get started. He's not happy that I wasn't tucked up in my own bed last night and I'm guessing that right about now he is blaming you."

"Not the first time that boy wasn't happy with me." Lee shrugged. "Come on let's get you home."

As I settled in the car and Lee started driving I noticed him looking sideways at me.

"What?" I asked.

"Last night you said you had issues with cars, are you okay?"

My face softened "I'm fine."

"Want to tell me what happened."

"Not much to tell. I was driving home when a drunk driver swerved onto my side of the road and hit my car. Woke up several days later unable to feel my legs."

Lee hissed his breath out.

"I don't remember anything about the actual accident. My Uncle Frank is a cop and he was first on the scene. He's told me about it. Held my hand while they were cutting me out of the car. Refused to leave me until my parents got to the hospital."

"Must have been tough on him," Lee commented. "Got to say, that was always a nightmare I had when I attended a car accident, that it'd be Jake or another kid I knew."

"Yeah, I didn't realize how much it affected him until his wife took me aside and told me about bad dreams he was having, about me not making it, or it being one of his kids. I don't complain anymore when he holds me a little too tight when he hugs me, or he's a little overprotective. I gave him an up close and personal vision of his nightmare."

"How long were you in hospital?"

"Not long, I was in rehab for a while though, learning how to walk again. I had bruising on my spine, that's why I couldn't feel my legs. It takes a while to get over that."

"You had heaps of support though right."

"With my family, you better believe it. I had my parents, of course, and my brother and sister, but there were also grandparents, aunts, uncles and cousins always on hand to help out."

"Anyone special there for you?"

My smile dimmed a bit. "My fiancé couldn't cope with my injuries. He left me after the accident."

"Gutless," Lee commented.

"No, he just didn't love me enough to take care of me if I ended up in a wheelchair."

"Must have hurt," Lee said gently.

"Like you would not believe. I thought I was totally destroyed but one day I'm lying in the hospital bed, with my Grandma Rita sitting in a chair beside me knitting away. I felt some pain in my leg, told my grandmother and promptly burst into tears and wailed something stupid about Paul and how he should be there. My grandmother basically told me that I had two choices, I could be sad or angry. If I was sad I should just give up because I wasn't going anywhere, anger would get me back on my feet. She told me to hold onto that anger."

"Would you take him back if he wanted you?"

"No," I said, relieved to know I meant it.

"Good to know." Lee stared straight ahead at the road.

I threw him a sideways glance. "I'm serious, Lee, you

cannot be matchmaking."

"But I like you and I think you would be good for Jake," Lee said.

My head dropped. "Flattering as that is to hear, you cannot start manipulating your son's love life just because you are feeling a bit clucky."

"Did you just call me clucky?" Lee sounded affronted.

"Yes, and if you're not careful you're going to become like one of those Italian mothers, constantly complaining that their kids haven't given them any grandchildren yet."

Lee looked insulted as he pulled up outside my building.

"It was good to meet you, Lee," I said as I got out of the car.

"You too," he said.

I waved as he pulled out of the driveway. Turning to head up to my apartment, I had Sean come running up to me, following me as I walked.

"Are you okay?" he asked.

"I'm fine," I said. "But I think you and I are going to need to have a little talk."

Sean hung his head and I couldn't help but feel sorry for him. Opening the door to the apartment, I motioned him towards the couch.

"So, are you going to tell my why you called Griffin this morning?" I asked gently.

Sean seemed to be having trouble meeting my eyes. "I came over early this morning to see you, before you went to work. You didn't answer the door so I opened it with my key and could see that you weren't here. I got worried and so I called Griffin."

I shook my head. "Okay, we're going to start with the beginning of that explanation because it raises a bunch of questions. First of all, why do you have a key to my place?"

"I do some work in the apartments at times. Miss Betsy gave me the master keys yesterday to do some work and I need to finish it today. Your key is on that group."

"Alright, though for future reference, could you at least please try to call me before entering my house next time? How did you know that I hadn't just left for work early?"

"Car was still in the parking area."

"Smart," I said. "Now for the next big question. Why on earth would you call Griffin? Your better bet would have been Miss Betsy, Crystal or Edwin, or maybe anyone other than Griffin. Believe me, having Griffin yelling at me through my phone was not a particularly pleasant way for me to begin the day."

"Sorry," said Sean. "It's just, when you got shot Griffin talked to me about it and he said if ever I was concerned about you that I should call him. He asked me to keep an eye on you for him."

"Sean," I said gently. I could see that my not being there had put fear in the boy's eyes. I could have kicked myself. Sean had been tossed out of home by his mother and her boyfriend. I had found him when he had been scared and alone, hiding behind a facade of bravado. Between myself and the other residents of the apartment complex we had given him a home, but I could still see that he was afraid of losing it. "I'm sorry I scared you," I said. "Yesterday was a bit of a chaotic day and I ended up somewhere I hadn't expected to be and fell asleep before I could head home. I was pretty exhausted."

"New boyfriend?" Sean asked curiously.

"No," I said. "If you must know Griffin abandoned me at his father's last night when he left me there during dinner."

"Then why was he so worried when I called when he knew where you were."

"His dad was supposed to take me straight home but it didn't work out that way. Next time you are worried about me, just call my cell. I don't care what time of the day or night it is, if you're worried, call me."

"Okay," said Sean.

"Now get going so I can clean up. The call from

Griffin freaked me out so much I came straight back here. I haven't had a chance to shower or anything."

"Yeah, I was wondering about that. You do smell a bit ripe," said Sean, a cheeky grin playing on his face.

"Nice. I can see you're going to be a hit with the ladies when you get older, considering all the charm I'm seeing now," I drawled, shooing him out of my apartment.

"Could be worse," Sean said. "Could be like Griffin."

I shivered theatrically, "Now that would just be cruel."

Hearing Sean laughing felt good. The kid had been given a rough ride in life and I enjoyed when I saw his face light up with a cheeky smile.

Chapter Eight

After getting ready for the day I contacted the hospital to find that Adele was finally able to have visitors. Arriving at the hospital I felt a strange shiver pass through me. Two months ago I had been in this same building after being shot by a murderer intent on hiding their crime, an experience that I never wanted to repeat. I had come out of the experience physically sound, but I still had some nights when I woke from a nightmare covered in sweat. Knocking on the door to Adele's room I heard her quiet voice call out for me to come in. Opening the door I saw Adele lying in the bed looking very frail. The private room had been made to look as little like a hospital room as it was possible to get. Near the window which looked out onto the carpark stood Adele's lawyer, Elliot Powell. His face was creased in concern and I could see that I had interrupted a discussion that he had been having with Adele.

Elliot's wife, Miranda Powell, sat next to Adele on the corner of the bed, looking through her medical chart. I was momentarily taken aback by the invasion of privacy until I remembered that Miranda was a plastic surgeon at one of the private hospitals. Miranda looked like the poster child of plastic surgery. She was one of those people who, even though she was in her late forties, she was looking fabulous, and believe me when I say that fabulous was the right word for her. Flawless skin, beautiful hair and a figure that could stop traffic, she looked like a woman who should be acting in movies next to the stars she operated on. I have to admit that between Miranda's stunning beauty and Adele's delicate looks I was feeling a little self-conscious, considering I hadn't even taken the time to do more than brush my hair, pull it back into my standard ponytail and throw on a minimal amount of makeup. Actually I should be honest with myself, it would take a lot more work than I was willing to endure to put me into the league of these two women.

"Oh, Trudie," Adele said, holding out her arm towards me. I gripped her hand and was surprised at the fragility that I felt in it.

"Are you alright, you poor thing. What you saw yesterday must have been so traumatic for you."

"I'm fine," I said, squeezing her hand.

"Can you tell us what happened?" Elliot interrupted. "The police aren't telling us anything other than Eric was found dead with Adele."

Miranda interrupted. "Surely this can wait until later. Adele has already been through so much, the last thing she needs is to hear about this."

Adele smiled at Miranda and patted her on the hand.

"I know you are trying to protect me, Randi, but I need to know what happened. The last thing I remember is going to bed, my bed, two nights ago. Next thing I know, I wake up here and they're telling me that Eric is dead. I need to know what happened."

"I can't tell you much," I said cautiously, desperately trying to work out what I could tell her. Adele was my client but I did not want to do anything which could compromise Griffin's investigation. "I arrived yesterday morning, the house was quiet so I went looking for you. I found you both in Eric's room, in bed together. There was blood on his side of the bed. I checked that you were breathing and then called for an ambulance. The police got there almost immediately and the ambulance was right behind them. After that I got taken to the police station. I was kept there for a while but I couldn't tell them anything more than that."

"So you didn't see anything else, a car leaving, anyone strange around the property?" Elliot asked.

"I'm sorry, there was nothing unusual except for the

house being quiet."

"I'm so glad that whoever did this wasn't still there when you walked in," Adele said, quietly squeezing my hand once again.

"I just wish you hadn't been there," said Miranda, tears in her eyes as she put an arm around Adele.

Elliot walked over and squeezed his wife's shoulder. Looking at them I remembered what Adele had told me about her lawyer and his wife. The three of them had known each other for years, along with Adele's first husband. They had gone through school together and always been a tight knit group. Adele had told me that she wouldn't have made it through the death of her first husband without their support. It looked like they were going to need to support her through the death of another husband.

Adele gave a small smile. "I need to talk to Trudie about some things. Could we have a few moments?"

Elliot and Miranda nodded and after both of them gave Adele a kiss on the cheek they left the room.

"Sit down here, Trudie," Adele said, patting the bed.

"What did you want to talk about?" I asked as I sat down.

"I'm going to be expected to organize the funeral for Eric," she said. I though the way she phrased that was interesting. "I need you to do that. I can't deal with any of this. I won't deal with it. Can you take care of it?"

"Of course I can," I said soothingly. "I need details on Eric's family so that I can coordinate with them."

"Eric never talked about his family but before we got married I had a private investigator look into his background. By the time the investigation started I had gone to Vegas with Eric and married him. By that point I didn't want Eric to find out what I had done, so I paid the investigator and told him to get rid of the file. He might still have some information."

"Do you have a name for me?" I asked, wanting

desperately to know how she could be so stupid as to have Eric investigated and not do anything about it.

Within the first few minutes of meeting the guy, every instinct in me had started blaring that there was something suspicious about him. It was too late to do anything about it now, we just had to deal with the fallout. Or rather, I was having to deal with the fallout. So far in my life I had never had to organize a funeral for a person. I had to organize a funeral for a pet pig for one of my clients once, I was hoping that some of the same concepts would apply.

"He's the one that BillieJo Freeman used before she got divorced. Do you know him?"

I shook my head. No I didn't, but Monique would. That was just the kind of information she would have. BillieJo Freeman had been the glamorous wife of famous NFL quarterback, Wayne Freeman. Everyone knew she was on the way out, and they also knew that she had a punishing prenup that was going to leave her with absolutely nothing. BillieJo hired some private detective and in no time she got her divorce with a very healthy payout and a groveling apology online from Wayne about how he did her wrong. Nobody knew what the investigator had found on Wayne, and BillieJo wasn't saying, but it must have been bad. That investigator then became the go to man in LA for anyone wanting to get the goods on a cheating spouse.

"I'll take care of it," I said confidently.

"Thank you, Trudie. You're such a treasure," Adele said as she lowered herself back on the bed and closed her eyes.

Recognizing a dismissal when I saw it, I murmured a quick goodbye and walked out. Outside the room I found Elliot and Miranda Powell waiting.

"Is she alright?" asked Miranda worriedly.

"I think she wants to sleep," I said.

The two of them looked at me expectantly as if they wanted me to tell them what she had talked about.

"Adele has asked me to organize the funeral for Eric," I said, turning to Elliot. "Do you have any information regarding what sort of service he would want or Adele would want? She hasn't really given me anything to work with."

"We didn't know Eric very well. Adele married him suddenly and she kept him away from us as much as possible," Elliot said.

I nodded understandingly. When you make a mistake, the last thing you want to do is flaunt that mistake in front of the people closest to you, and Adele's mistake had been huge.

Chapter Nine

Walking into Monique's office, I realized that maybe I should have called ahead and given her a heads up about what had happened to my latest client. I was surprised to find my friend, Edwin, sitting at the reception desk of Monique's office. He was talking on the phone and actually put a finger up to stop me from saying anything.

"I know you really need someone but unfortunately we don't have anyone available at this moment. I will put you on the list but I can't promise anything." Edwin winced.

"They hung up on you didn't they?" I said as he put down the phone.

"They did," he said, his very proper English accent sounding out of place.

"What are you doing working here?" I asked him.

"Need the money," he said. "And Monique loves the way I sound on the phone." He grimaced.

Monique was right, Edwin had a divine voice for the phone. A proper English accent but a deep voice that women found intoxicating. He was an aspiring actor and had moved to LA looking for his big break. He had everything, the movie star good looks, the beautiful voice and the soulful eyes that just screamed out that he needed to be in one of those romantic movies. The only problem was, the man could not act to save his life. I had seen him in a play in some very out of the way theater. It was almost painful to watch. Modeling he could do, and had done to support himself, but it just wasn't enough for him. He wanted to be something more than a model and decided acting was for him. In the meantime, Edwin took on jobs to supplement his income. He had met Monique when she was at my place once and she sometimes offered him work when it was available.

"How do you deal with these people all the time, Trudie?" he asked. "They are rude and demanding and I just couldn't do your job."

"You're too pretty to do my job," I said. "You'd have women climbing all over you in no time."

Edwin blushed. That right there was why he was wrong for the movie and modeling business. The man still blushed when somebody complimented him.

"Is she in?" I asked.

"Yes she is and she looks free at the moment. I'll buzz you in."

Walking into Monique's office I could see Monique getting off the phone from Edwin and greeting me with that smile of hers. Monique's office reflected her perfectly, elegant without being overdone. I had met Monique Petit during a particularly trying job as a nanny in London. She had been impressed by the way that I dealt with an unusual and stressful situation, and had recruited me for her agency. When I first met Monique I had been impressed with the way that she held herself when she walked into the room. A tall beautiful dark skinned woman, she commanded attention everywhere she went. Monique is who I want to be when I finally get around to growing up. She never lets anything stop her. She is the ultimate slash person. That is model/actress/businesswoman/real estate mogul. Monique has never let anything get in her way and has created her own little empire. The agency I work for is only one part of her kingdom.

"How are things going with Adele and Eric?" she said as I sat down.

I looked startled, sure she would have heard. Usually her information is impeccable.

"Eric was murdered yesterday morning," I said slowly.

"I hadn't heard," Monique said, "I flew in from France yesterday so I've been a bit out of the loop. What happened?"

"I'm not sure," I replied. "I walked into their house yesterday morning when I got to work and found both Adele and Eric in bed. Eric was dead and Adele was passed out. I called the police and spent most of yesterday dealing with that. I should have called you but I kind of got caught up with it all."

"Do you need Reggie?" Monique asked.

Reggie Goodman is Monique's husband and one of the best lawyers in LA. I have used Reggie during previous encounters with the LAPD. Reggie is almost the physical opposite to Monique but the two of them are devoted to one another.

"I think I've got it under control. I haven't been threatened with arrest or deportation yet, so I'm doing better than usual," I replied wryly.

Monique nodded, smiling.

"One thing though, Adele has asked me to organize the funeral for Eric. It's a little out of my comfort zone so I'm not really sure who to contact."

Monique pulled out a card and passed it to me. "This is Tomas, he organizes funeral events, memorials, all those kinds of things. Whatever you need he will be able to do it."

Holding the card I mulled over the fact that I had never in my life realized that anyone other than a funeral director organized funerals. Sometimes it hit me how far away I was from home and this was one of those moments.

"Also, I need to know the name of the private investigator in the BillieJo Freeman divorce case."

"Why would you need to know that?" Monique asked curiously.

"Adele used him to get information on Eric when she first started seeing him, but ended up doing the quickie Vegas wedding thing before the investigation was finished. She never ended up getting the file, because she felt that it was a betrayal of her wedding vows to look into his background. Now though, she wants to let his family know and invite them to the funeral."

Monique just looked at me.

"Yes I know," I said. "Bad decisions all round in that situation."

"Well if she used the same investigator as BillieJo, that would be Travis Cooper." Monique quickly looked at her computer and wrote down some details on a piece of paper. "He's very good at his job. I've never needed to use him but I know Reggie has in some of his cases. It does take a bit to see him. From what I understand he is very busy and has a waiting list a mile long. It could take you a while to get an appointment."

"I need to get in pretty much immediately," I said.

"I'll call Reggie and see what he can do," Monique said, smiling gently.

Chapter Ten

Walking into Travis Cooper's office I was quite surprised. Brought up on a diet of noir films I expected a PI to have a dingy office in some out of the way office block, in a bad part of town. Travis Cooper's office shared a building with lawyer's offices and was light, airy and modern. The receptionist sitting on the front desk was not an up and coming actress who was filling in time until her big break which is what I saw very often. She was an older woman who looked like she was everyone's favorite grandmother. I walked up to her with a smile on my face and as friendly a look as I could manage. My mother taught me that you always treat the front desk staff the best and that will make your life so much easier.

"Hi, my name is Trudie Eyre. I've got an appointment to see Mr Cooper. Thank you so much for getting me in at such short notice."

The older woman blushed. I recognized that blush. Reggie was absolutely devoted to Monique but when he put on the charm, he could get women to do anything he wanted. It looked like Travis Cooper's receptionist was just as susceptible as the rest of the women in LA. At that point a tall man barreled out of the office and stopped short just before running into me.

"I'll be out for a bit, Maria," he said as he adjusted the backpack on his shoulder. "Just got word on the Johnson case."

"Don't you dare," Maria said with a bit of bite. "I just told you that you have an appointment. You are not running out now. Reggie Goodman sent her."

"I'm sorry, miss." Travis Cooper turned to me and I felt the full force of those brown chocolate eyes. I steadied my legs as I could feel myself about to melt into a puddle. I live in LA and a lot of the time I am surrounded by very attractive men. I have attended parties and premieres with men who are regularly voted some of the hottest on the planet and not been impressed, but Travis Cooper was gorgeous.

"Adele Wesson sent me to talk to you about her husband, Eric," I said hurriedly.

"Knew that mess was going to end badly," Cooper muttered. "Okay, I'll talk to you but you need to come with me and we need to move it now."

I wanted to ask where we were going, but he was already out the door.

I looked at Maria and she smiled encouragingly. "He won't wait, you need to follow him and don't let him out of your sight."

I raced off after him and caught up at the elevators where he was impatiently hitting the button. The trip in the elevator was silent and I could feel his eyes on me as if evaluating me. His car was a generic one which surprised me, a little beaten up, it would have faded into the background anywhere, but I guess that is why he used it. Cooper efficiently navigated the streets of LA and in no time we were parked outside of a hotel in an area I had never been before.

As he was getting his camera out Cooper started talking. "So you're one of Monique's people." He looked me over. "You definitely look the type." I raised an eyebrow and he chuckled. "So you've been working for Adele Wesson. That must have been fun."

"Adele is a lovely person to work for," I said defensively.

"The woman is an idiot," Cooper said. I sucked in my breath to tell him off and he raised his hand. "I'm not saying that to be mean. She's a rich woman, newly widowed and she has this young guy sniffing around her. Does she stop to think what his angle is? No, she jumps in his bed and then takes him to Vegas and marries him."

"They could have been in love," I said quietly. "Not everyone has to have an angle."

"Honey, everyone's got an angle, everyone's out for themselves. Do you have any idea the number of fairy tale weddings that end up with me, sitting in this clunker of a car, aiming a telephoto lens at someone who is sleeping with someone other than the person they vowed before God or state that they would love forever?"

I tried to interrupt but he was obviously on a roll.

"People get so caught up in finding 'the one', and then they decide 'the one' irritates them, and instead of working it out they start looking for a new 'the one'. Marriage isn't forever anymore. In fact, if I didn't make so much money out of it, I would be saying that the whole institution should be banned."

"Finished?" I asked as he took a breath. "Because fascinating as your opinion on the state of modern marriage is, I am really trying to get some information for Adele. Eric is dead and I am supposed to be organizing the funeral for him. Adele was hoping that in your investigation that you may have found if he had any family who should be attending the funeral."

"Eric is dead?" asked Cooper.

"Yes, he was killed yesterday morning."

"How?"

"From what I could see it looked like something hit his head and made a mess. I don't know if it was a bullet or something big and heavy but there was a lot of blood on the pillow."

Cooper aimed the large camera in his hand at the hotel lobby doors and started adjusting the lens.

"So," he said, in what he obviously believed was an offhand manner. "Were you sleeping with him?"

"Why does everyone ask that question? No I wasn't sleeping with him, I had never slept with him and I didn't want to sleep with him."

"You gay?" Cooper asked. "Nothing wrong with that, some of my best fantasies involve gay women."

I looked at him in disgust. "You are truly unpleasant to talk to, has anyone told you that?"

"Often," he said smiling, showing his straight white teeth.

"I am not gay. I did not sleep with him. Why don't we just put it down to me being one of those idiots who believes in the whole marriage vows being sacred thing?"

"An idealist," Cooper said. "That's great." He fished into his pocket and took out a card and pushed it into a side pocket of my purse. "You keep this in your wallet and when you find 'the one' and get that feeling that he isn't so keen on his vows, you give me a call. I'll give you a discount rate."

I went against every part of my upbringing and refused to thank him.

"So, what can you tell me about Eric?"

"Eric Wesson," he drawled. "You know he took her name, told her he was doing it to honor her first marriage, to prove how much he loved her. Grew up in LA with his mother. No idea who the father was. The kid was smart but didn't get much of a chance at school. That's about as far as I got before Adele went and married the guy and pulled the plug on the investigation."

"You didn't go any further with it?" I asked curiously.

"Honey, I don't run a charity and I sure as hell don't run a counseling service. People are responsible for their own stupid decisions. It wasn't my job to tell her that she'd married the wrong guy."

I was about to say something when his attention was caught on the front door of the hotel.

"Well, well, well. Looks like Mr Johnson has not been taking his marriage vows seriously either."

"He could be having a meeting in there," I said indignantly. "You don't know for sure."

"Honey," Cooper said patiently as he was clicking away

with his camera. "Could you give me one good reason that Mr Johnson would leave his office in the middle of the day, with his secretary and go to an out of the way hotel for a meeting. By the way, I know for a fact this place does not have conference facilities."

I was silent. I couldn't think of a reason and frankly if he was running around cheating on his wife, it wasn't my business to defend him.

"So," Cooper said, still snapping away at the hapless couple while I was trying very hard not to notice that Mr Johnson's trouser zipper was still undone. Cooper winked at me. He knew I'd seen the same thing he had. "You found the body."

I nodded, not game to answer.

"Get pulled in by the cops for questioning?" he asked.

"Yes," I said.

"Know the name of the cops who pulled you in."

"Jake Griffin and Liza Ramos," I said. I was looking at him so I noticed the stormy look in his eyes at the mention of Griffin's name.

"You know Griffin," I ventured.

"Yes," said Cooper. "He was my partner when I first made it to detective, before I left the force."

"Doesn't sound like there are fond memories," I said, watching him carefully.

"Let's just say that I learned that it was better to rely on myself than to depend on someone else," Cooper said.

"Someone else being Griffin?" I persisted.

"Kind of nosy aren't you?" Cooper said as he tucked the camera back in the bag and started up the car.

"Just a little curious," I said, trying to be casual but I could see that Cooper was able to see right through me.

"Oh, honey," he said. "Let me give you a piece of advice. Jake Griffin lives and breathes the LAPD. Nothing and no one comes before it. If you have set your sights on him then you are going to be sadly disappointed. There will come a day when you will ask him to put you first, to believe in you and back you up. On that day he will leave you and you will realize that you are better off without him."

"What did he do?" I asked, any pretense at being disinterested a vague memory.

"None of your business, sweetheart. Let's just say I learned too late that just because he was my partner didn't mean he had my back. On that day I had a choice whether to stay in the LAPD and put up with that kind of thing, or strike out on my own, where I know that I only have myself to depend on."

Getting to his office Cooper turned to me. "I have everything I got for Adele Wesson upstairs," he said.

I followed him quietly, still digesting his words over Griffin. To be perfectly honest he wasn't saying anything that I wasn't already aware of. Since I'd met him, Griffin had repeatedly proved to me that his job came first. Maybe I was reading too much into the kiss that happened in the hospital. The fact the guy hadn't contacted me in the last two months seemed to be a good indication of where I was on his level of priorities. After my broken engagement I had realized that I wasn't going to be happy with just getting out there again. If I was going to risk my heart again I was going to go for awesome. I didn't intend to settle for anything less. Smiling at Maria as we passed her desk, I was quiet as I followed Cooper. Reaching into his filing cabinet he pulled out a pretty thin file and passed it to me.

"There's everything that I have on Eric Wesson. Like I said, Adele pulled the plug before I could really get into it, but I did hear that he had a mother that he didn't really speak to. Almost felt sorry for the poor guy once I heard a bit about her. Made me think that he might actually be looking for a mother figure in Adele and not just her money."

"Oh that's a pleasant thought," I grimaced.

"Takes all types, sweetheart," Cooper said, smiling.

"Even deluded romantics waiting for their Prince Charming."

I decided not to answer that, knowing that I was being counted amongst the deluded romantics.

"Thank you, Mr Cooper," I said. "If we need any more information are you available for further work for Adele?"

"Actually, sweetheart, I am kind of busy at the moment, my reputation being what it is." Cooper sat down and leaned back in his chair. "But if you would be willing to call me Travis and you were the one doing the calling, I might be convinced."

"Why?" I asked incredulously.

"Let's just say that with my line of work, sometimes it's refreshing to be around a deluded romantic."

I sighed. I could never understand why I attracted the weird ones.

"Fine, Travis, If I call and ask very nicely and let you laugh at my foolish dreams will you help me?"

"If you put it that way, how could I possibly refuse?" He held out his hands, palms up and had such an innocent look on his face that I couldn't stop the laugh that came out of me.

In that instant Travis's face changed and his eyes looked like melted chocolate. "Sweetheart," he said, "you really should laugh more often. That smile could stop traffic."

I stopped laughing, feeling self-conscious all of a sudden. I was the wallflower, I was used to that role. Compliments from gorgeous men really didn't usually come my way. Suddenly nervous I held out my hand to shake his.

"Thank you very much for your help."

Travis stood up and his hand engulfed mine. I noticed how small my hand looked next to his. His deep tan in stark contrast to the paleness of my skin.

He kept a hold of my hand until I looked up. "Anytime you need any help," he said, looking at me intently. "Just give me a call."

"Thank you," I mumbled, pulled my hand back and quickly made my exit.

As I left the office I looked back to see Travis watching me from his doorway with a thoughtful expression on his face. I finally took a breath once I had left the office building. Travis Cooper unnerved me in a way that I really wasn't used to.

Chapter Eleven

B ack in my car I pulled out the card Monique had given me and dialed the number.

"Everlasting Events, Tomas speaking." I looked at the phone in shock.

The voice on the end of the phone was not what I was expecting from someone that organized funeral services. The voice was male but with a high pitched, excited quality to it that I wasn't sure fit with what I assumed was the somber nature of the job. I had obviously let the silence go for too long because the voice started up again.

"It's okay, take your time. I'll just wait until you're ready to talk."

"Uh no, that's fine. My name is Trudie Eyre. I was given your card by Monique Petit. I am organizing a funeral service for the husband of my client and Monique suggested that you would be the best person to help me."

"Of course," Tomas said smoothly. "When are you available to meet?"

"I'm available whenever you are," I said, crossing my fingers. The sooner I sorted out this mess, the happier I was going to be.

"I can meet you now for a coffee," Tomas said and named a small coffee shop that I knew.

Sitting in the coffee shop half an hour later, I realized that I had no idea what he looked like. I hate meeting someone I don't know. Every time the door opened I swiveled my head around and tried to work out whether the person coming through was the person that I was supposed to meet. I shouldn't have worried. When Tomas Burnelli walked in I could see that he matched his voice perfectly. I raised my hand. He saw me and headed my way. Tomas Burnelli was a slight man with delicate features. His demeanor screamed an interesting personality. His tanned skin and brown eyes denoted an Italian heritage, but his hair had been dyed a strong platinum blond, providing a stark contrast to his countenance. His eyes twinkled with a barely suppressed joy. Looking at him you would assume that he would be best suited in the most flamboyant of colors. Unfortunately, in obvious deference to his work, he wore a dull gray suit matched with a lovely leather man bag that he wore slung across his body. The whole look made me think of a peacock with a blanket thrown over it. You can see fabulous is there, it is peeking out of the sides, but it is being completely smothered. I stood as he approached and he held out his arms, grabbed my shoulders and kissed me on the cheek.

"Trudie," he said, his voice carrying to the rest of the coffee shop. "It is so good to meet you."

I motioned for him to sit down and we ordered our coffees. Tomas looked at me with that irrepressible twinkle in his eye.

"So, Trudie, how can I help you?"

"I have a client, her husband passed away rather suddenly yesterday."

"Wait, wait," Tomas said. "I must write all this down. He pulled an ornate leather bound notebook from his bag and settled it on the table. "Very well," he said. "Keep going."

"As I said, my client's husband passed away quite suddenly yesterday in less than optimal circumstances. My client is well known but not overly famous, so there may be some media interest. We are looking for a discreet and tasteful way of holding the funeral. Is this something you would be able to do?" I asked, holding my breath.

"Of course I can do it," Tomas said quietly. I was pleased to see that the voice that had previously carried to all ends of the coffee shop, could be modulated for privacy when required. "The issue we have is that I need to have all the information if I am to do the job properly."

I looked at him, loath to give this information to someone that I had only just met. Tomas sighed, obviously aware of my internal dilemma. "Would it make it any easier for you, Trudie, if I told you that I used to work for Monique as one of her personal assistants?"

"Really?" I asked.

"Yes, really. I was with Monique for four years and had various clients, all of whom were challenging but interesting which I'm sure is the same way you ended up here today."

"Why did you leave?" I asked curiously.

"I had always wanted to be an events planner. Working with Monique's clients honed those skills and I ended up branching out on my own."

"As a funeral events planner?" I said questioningly. Not exactly a career path that I had envisaged.

Tomas smiled. "Not exactly at first. I started off working as a wedding planner."

That made sense. I could see the man in front of me being a wedding planner, he would be perfect in the role.

"Why don't you still do that?" I asked.

"Brides," Tomas shivered. "Some women can be truly vicious on their wedding day. I got tired of dealing with women who were determined to reduce everyone around them to tears. The last wedding that I did was a nightmare. The mother of the groom died in the middle of the planning stage for the wedding. The bride was too busy with wedding plans to help with the organization of the funeral of the mother of the man she supposedly loved. He asked me to help and I felt so sorry for the guy that I organized the funeral for him. He was so grateful for the work I did, while his bride-to-be did nothing but raise the stress levels of everyone around her."

"That was a good thing you did," I said gently.

Tomas smiled at me. "I got more joy and a stronger feeling that I had helped people that day than I ever did for any of the weddings I planned, so I changed my focus. I no longer plan the best day of people's lives, I help them get through one of the worst."

I felt tears prick the back of my eyes. "That is lovely," I said. "I've never looked at it that way."

Tomas looked embarrassed. "On the plus side, the groom got smart. He dumped the bitch he was going to marry at the funeral, when she turned up drunk in a tiny red dress that left nothing to the imagination."

"My image of happy ever after is taking a battering today," I muttered.

"Why?" asked Tomas.

"I met a PI today who spends his life following people around while they cheat on their spouses and now, you. I'm beginning to think that marriage is a recipe for disaster."

"It usually is," said Tomas. "So are you ready to trust me with some of the details that I am going to need for your client's husband?"

"Okay," I said. "My client is Adele Wesson." Tomas nodded in recognition. "Her second husband, Eric, who she married a year ago, was yesterday found dead in his bed. At this stage there are no details but there was a lot of blood."

Tomas nodded, frantically writing down information.

"As a result of all that blood there is a murder investigation happening. The police have control of Eric's body right now and at this stage I am not sure when it is going to be released. Adele is currently in hospital and I am not sure when she will be discharged, so that is another thing we have to be sure of before organizing the service. I am currently in the process of trying to find out about any other family for Eric who may want to be involved in the funeral. I will contact you if I get any more information from that investigation. We want the funeral to be discreet, possibly in an out of the way place which is difficult for the media to get to. Usually Adele isn't famous enough for the major media coverage that celebrities get but, because of the way that Eric died, I am a bit concerned that they may try to put a bit of a sensationalist spin on it."

"Understandable," Tomas said. "Any thought on whether he was religious."

I almost choked. The thought of bacchanalian Eric following a pious religion was almost laughable.

"I doubt it but I will let you know if his family has anything to say about that."

"I will need to know the kind of music wanted and whether anyone will be doing a eulogy. I know a minister, she's pretty good regarding services. Especially if there is the potential for issues such as conflict between family members, that sort of thing. I know a funeral home and cemetery that is out of the way which we could use."

"I will see what information I can get together in the next couple of days for you," I said.

"Most importantly, I will need to know when the police will release the body so we at least have a day to work with it," Tomas said.

Thinking of Griffin, I said, "I may be able to get that information. I'll give you a call."

"That sounds great," said Tomas, closing his notebook. "Oh, one more question, will it be an open or closed casket?"

I thought back to the previous morning. "I'm going to say a closed casket." I grimaced remembering the amount of blood that I had seen on Eric's pillow.

"Very well," said Tomas as he stood and held out his hand. I grasped it, grateful for his steady confidence.

"Thank you very much for your help."

"My pleasure," said Tomas. "As soon as you get more information could you please let me know. Also, if you want me to meet with other family members I would be happy to do that."

On my way to the hospital to meet with Adele again, I started thinking about Tomas. Since leaving Australia I hadn't really thought about a career path. To be perfectly honest I had fallen into my job with Monique. I loved doing it but I wasn't really sure whether I wanted to spend my life catering to the sometimes crazy whims of the rich and spoiled. Sooner or later I was going to snap and that would not end well. Monique liked me and I knew that she was patient with a lot of the things that her PAs threw her way. She hadn't turned a hair when I'd told her I had found my second body while at work. Sooner or later though she might lose some of that patience. Maybe I should be looking at my options in case that happened.

Chapter Twelve

Adele's hospital room seemed to be abuzz with activity. Nurses were coming in and out of the room, and Miranda Powell seemed to be directing them with all the efficiency of a general directing troops.

"What's happening?" I asked as I cautiously entered the room, dodging one nurse who looked particularly harried.

Miranda was the one who answered me while Adele sat serenely on the side of the bed.

"Adele wants to go home and there is nothing physically wrong with her, so we are organizing her discharge."

Adele didn't seem to be paying any attention to what was going on around her, so I was assuming the 'we' Miranda was referring to was herself as she took some paperwork from one of the nurses.

Sitting next to Adele I leaned over. "Are you sure you're ready to leave the hospital?"

I was a bit concerned as her eyes seemed to be a little unfocused. Adele always seemed to be a little vague and the wider questions of the world never seemed to affect her. Even so, she was looking a little more spaced out than I had ever seen her before.

Miranda looked over. "She's fine. She's still got some of the medications in her system but I'm going to take care of her for the next couple of days, make sure there are no lasting effects."

I felt better knowing that Miranda was involved. First aid was the extent of my medical training. A requirement of Monique's, considering the number of her staff who had needed to utilize that skill for suspected drug overdoses.

"Where will she be staying?" I asked.

"At her home," said Miranda.

I must have looked as horrified as I felt.

"Adele is fine with that," she said hurriedly.

Looking at the dilated pupils of Adele's eyes, I was pretty sure she would be fine with walking off the edge of the Grand Canyon. It didn't mean it was a particularly good idea though.

"Have you thought that maybe the police would be still interested in the house as a crime scene," I said slowly. "Maybe it would be better to put her in a suite at a hotel for a little while."

"But I need my clothes, my computer, my things," Adele said in an almost childish, sing song voice.

"I can get all of that for you," I said calmly, patting her on the shoulder but looking at Miranda, knowing that she was the one that I was going to need to convince.

Whatever medication Adele was on at the moment meant that she was in no way capable of making decisions. I knew in those circumstances Miranda and Elliot were going to be taking on the caring role. They were the ones that I was going to need to negotiate with to help Adele.

Miranda took a moment. "If you really think that is for the best, you are the only one of us who has seen the house since the incident."

"I really think that Adele is not ready for the house based on the last time I saw it," I said.

Miranda nodded. "Very well, if you can organize a suite for her to stay at and then get some clothes and anything else you think she will need, then I will take her to the hotel and we will meet you there."

"Will there be anyone staying with her?" I asked.

"I have hired a nursing agency that I use sometimes for my patients who prefer not to stay at hospital." Miranda smiled. "She will have a nurse with her twenty-four hours a day."

I nodded, encouraged that Adele was being well taken care of. Stepping out of the room I organized a hotel suite for Adele and then called the police station looking for permission to enter Adele's house. I was put through to Detective Ramos.

"We're finished with it," she said. "Did you want me to put you through to Griffin?"

Cooper's words were still ringing in my ears so I declined and hurriedly got off the phone.

"The hotel is sorted," I said as I entered Adele's room. "I've got the go ahead to access the house so I'll get everything I need for Adele. Is there anything in particular I should bring?"

"My laptop," said Adele. "And my notes. I think I know where I've been going wrong. It's all so much clearer now."

"I'll do that," I smiled.

Nodding to Miranda I left the room. Adele's house looked very much as it always did. Though it was not as opulent as some homes in LA, it had a peaceful coziness about it. Adele had once told me she could not part with the house when she became successful because she and her first husband had bought it together. She had always been happiest in this house. I wondered how Eric's death was going to affect that feeling of peace. The house showed definite signs of being searched by the police. Things were out of place, some items had been broken. I knew that I would need to try to recapture that serenity that Adele cherished before I could even think of allowing her back into the house. Just one more of the jobs I was going to need to do.

In Adele's room I grabbed some clothes and underwear. In the state she was in at the moment I didn't expect her to be overly fussy about the clothes I chose. I found Adele's laptop and notebooks that she used in the safe in her bedroom closet. Adele was a bit flaky about a lot of things but she was very much aware that her writing was important. She always took great care with her research and her laptop. I had been given the combination to the floor safe in the closet when I first started, with the knowledge that the second I left her employ the combination would be changed. As far as I knew Eric had never known the combination to the safe.

Heading to the hotel I had booked, I found Adele with the nurse. Miranda was talking on her cell out on the balcony so I sat next to Adele.

"How are you feeling?" I asked gently.

"Good," she said, frowning as if to concentrate. "Did you get my things?"

"Yes, I did," I said. "I've spoken to the investigator about Eric's family and I'll try to talk to them tomorrow. I've also started to organize the funeral service."

"That's good," she said, gripping my hand. "I'm glad you're here to help me."

"Are you going to need me for anything else tomorrow?" I asked.

"No, I just need you to take care of the funeral. At this point nothing else matters. I don't want to have to think about it," she looked at me pleadingly.

"I'll take care of everything," I said. "You just concentrate on getting better."

She nodded and walked towards her bedroom. I watched her walk away, my concern evident on my face.

"She's very fragile," said Miranda as she walked in from the balcony. "Always has been. Andrew used to be able to deal with her. I thought we were going to lose her when he died."

"Her first husband," I said.

"Yes, Andrew adored her and he let her be fragile and delicate. Adele never had to stand on her own two feet because Andrew took care of everything. When he died she fell apart. Elliot and I tried to fill the void but we could never be to her what Andrew was. When Eric came into her life he was passionate and exciting. We all knew he was a mistake but he gave her the first spark of life that we had seen since Andrew's death. I don't think any of us actually believed that she would marry him or else we would have tried to step in sooner," Miranda said regretfully.

"Do you think she'll be okay after this?" I asked.

"We'll get her through," Miranda said confidently. "It will just take some time and a lot of patience. I don't think it has got through to her that not only is Eric dead but the way he died. They're going to look at her for the murder and I don't know how she is going to deal with that. I don't think she is strong enough."

I couldn't refute what Miranda was saying. Adele was the wife in an unhappy marriage and she was the only one in the house when Eric was killed.

"I'll be working on the funeral tomorrow but I'll come by if I can to check on her," I said to Miranda.

"That would be good," Miranda smiled. "I know she likes you. Staffing has been a bit of a problem with Eric being, well Eric. You're the first one that she thought was going to last the distance."

I shrugged because really what could I say. It was kind of sad that the thing that I had going most for me was that I hadn't slept with her husband.

Chapter Thirteen

By the time I pulled up into my parking spot at my apartment I could feel myself starting to drift. It had been a long couple of days and I was looking forward to getting some sleep. Spotting Sean taking out his trash I called over and asked whether he wanted some dinner. I didn't really feel like cooking but I knew that a teenage boy was always hungry. It seemed to take both my and Miss Betsy's pantries to keep Sean fed.

"That's okay," he waved back. "I've already eaten. Goodnight, Trudie."

Very well then, quiet night in it was. I had to admit I was kind of looking forward to it. Coming up to the door of my apartment I realized that my quiet night was not going to happen. Detective Jake Griffin was leaning against the wall next to my door with a bag of what smelled like Thai food in his hands.

He held it up. "I figured I owed you for cutting out so quickly last night."

"You mean during my kidnapping?" I asked.

"It was dinner, not a kidnapping."

"Choices were taken away, that constitutes kidnapping."

"You are so stubborn," he said.

"My mother calls it strong willed," I said automatically.

"Are you going to let me in?" Griffin asked, holding the Thai food just out of my reach as an enticement.

"You're lucky I can't be bothered cooking tonight," I mumbled, opening the door and motioning for him to follow me.

I pulled out some plates and cutlery, placed them on the coffee table and sat on the couch with a groan.

"Busy day?" asked Griffin as he pulled out the

containers of food and opened them up. The aroma was heavenly and I started to serve myself a healthy helping.

"You could say that. I've been asked to organize Eric's funeral."

Griffin grimaced. "That doesn't sound very pleasant."

"Not particularly, but considering that Adele isn't really in much of a state to do anything, the rest of us are having to take up the slack."

My cell started ringing and I fished it out of my bag. It was Miranda. "I'm sorry to disturb you at home," she started, "but Adele is saying there were some photos in her notes that are missing. She's quite adamant."

"I got everything out of the safe that I could find that was relevant." I said. "There were some bags in the bottom of the safe but I assumed they were jewelry. I didn't want to go poking around in there. I can go back tomorrow if you want me to and give it a better look."

"That would be good," said Miranda. "She's quite distressed and I'm going to give her something so she can get to sleep."

I hung up the phone. Frankly I thought that the last thing Adele needed was further medication, but what did I know. Miranda was a respected doctor and I was the personal assistant who still looked up the internet whenever I got sick and managed to convince myself I was going to die from the common cold. Looking up I found Griffin staring at the business card that had fallen out of my bag when I pulled my cell phone out.

"Why are you dealing with Travis Cooper?" he asked.

I grabbed the card out of his hand. "He helped me out with an issue at work."

"Cooper deals with cheating husbands and wives," Griffin said. "Considering his history I'm assuming we're talking about Eric Wesson."

"Are we talking here or are you asking questions expecting me to answer?" I asked as I took a mouthful of food.

Griffin looked at me carefully. I could see him mentally stepping back. "We're just talking," he said.

I put my plate down. "I'm organizing the funeral. Adele doesn't know of any family that Eric might have but I think it is important for them to be given the chance to be there. Cooper had done some work for Adele previously, so I went to him for help."

"I just think you would be better off working with someone other than Cooper," Griffin said.

"Is this because of his reputation or based on what you know about him personally?" I asked.

Griffin looked surprised. "He told you about me?" he asked.

"Not really," I said. "Just that you used to work together."

I knew I was keeping some of the conversation to myself but I didn't feel that he needed to know everything that Travis had told me.

"Cooper is someone you should be very wary about dealing with," Griffin said in a measured tone.

Good to know that they both had the same level of distrust for each other.

"Your father seems nice," I said, thinking a change of topic was in order.

Griffin grunted while he was eating. Obviously not one of the topics to approach him with. The sound of his phone ringing interrupted us.

"Sorry," Griffin said as he got up.

I returned to my food, because seriously, it was that good. Griffin came back, an apologetic look on his face.

"I've got to get going," he said. "Just caught another case."

"If I spend much more time with you, I'll get to the point where I'll be too afraid to walk out my front door," I said.

"I like that you're thinking of spending more time with me," Griffin said softly, his eyes warming as he moved towards me.

As his lips touched mine I could feel myself melting against him. His arms came around me and I wound my arms around his shoulders, attempting to keep myself from falling to the floor as my knees gave out. Griffin pulled away and smiled into what I was sure were my flushed features.

"I'll see you soon," he said as he opened my door, gave me another quick kiss on the lips and disappeared.

I closed my door and leaned heavily against it. I was in so much trouble. I had a feeling that I was in no way capable of handling Jake Griffin, and that kiss was stamped with a great deal of possessiveness to it. I was serious when I said that I wasn't willing to settle for anything other than awesome. I had a very bad feeling that Jake Griffin was capable of breaking my heart, and the worst part was, he wouldn't even mean to do it.

Chapter Fourteen

The next morning as I looked blearily into my mirror after a restless night of tossing and turning in my bed, I roundly cursed all hot detectives and the way my heart seemed to race a little every time I thought of Detective Griffin. The last thing I needed right now was to get involved with a man that tied up in his work. Rightly or wrongly, I wanted someone who would always put me first, just like my grandmother told me I deserved. After my ex-fiancée had dumped me, my Grandma Rita had been a very regular feature in my rehabilitation room while I learned to walk again. One day, when things had started getting on top of me she had told me that I deserved amazing, that my ex was a moron, that I didn't need him and I should pull up my big girl panties and grab life. Of course she had ruined her little feminist power speech by then telling me she hoped those panties weren't the beige full briefs that she knew I wore, because men liked a bit of silk and lace and there wasn't any harm in always being prepared. My grandmother always had very interesting views on things which she was never afraid to share with her grandchildren.

The heavy knocking on my front door interrupted my musing. I opened it to find my friend, Crystal, peering over my shoulder while handing me a coffee.

"He's not here," I said dryly, turning around as she followed.

"Pity," Crystal said. "I was at least hoping to get a glimpse of Detective Hottie as he walked out of the shower."

"Really," I said.

"I figured that considering those black circles under your eyes that at least you had some very good, or very hot stories to tell me to justify what is obviously a severe lack of sleep."

"That bad, huh?" I asked.

"Trudie, you look like a panda bear whose mascara is running."

I looked at her sourly as Crystal sipped her coffee serenely. I liked Crystal but then I was able to handle her sometimes brutal honesty. I knew of many other people who weren't quite so understanding. My ringing phone interrupted what was obviously going to be Crystal starting her favorite topic, of why I should be enjoying my youth, and scoring with every good looking man I saw. I loved the girl but she was a prime example of how having the wrong parents could really mess you up. Although I liked her dad, he was nice. Crystal's mother on the other hand was the most selfish human being I had ever met in my life. Considering my job and the people I came into contact with on a regular basis, that was actually saying something. The phone call was Adele and I was pleased to note that she sounded to be a lot more with it than she had been yesterday. I hoped that meant that she had wound down the number of drugs she was taking.

"Trudie, I just heard from the police," she said nervously. "They said that I can collect Eric's body and get him ready for burial. I can't deal with it." I could hear the tears hitching in her voice.

"I have it all under control," I said soothingly. "When did you want to have the funeral?"

"Can it be tomorrow?" she asked. "I just want it over and done with."

A little harsh I thought, considering the man in question was her husband for almost a year but this was my job.

"I'll see what I can do," I said. "I'll organize the details today and get in touch with you this afternoon to let you know."

"Thank you, Trudie. I don't know what I would have

done without you through this horrible ordeal."

Getting off the phone I realized that I was going to have to do some fancy footwork today to make sure everything was organized for a funeral tomorrow. First job was calling Tomas. Explaining the situation to him I was relieved when he assured me that twenty-four hours' notice for a funeral was not only achievable but barely a challenge.

I hung up the phone and Crystal peered at me.

"Going to be a bad day?" she asked sympathetically.

"It's Eric Wesson's funeral tomorrow and I need to find out if any of his family are able to go."

"Any leads?" she asked.

"I've got a file from a PI that Adele used to investigate him but it's incomplete as she married him before the investigation was finished."

Crystal gave me a look.

I sighed. "I know, sometimes I wonder about her too. It's got an old employer listed here. It's a gym, maybe I'll go there and find out whether they've got any family on file for him."

"Do you want some company?" Crystal asked.

"Don't you have to work today?" I asked curiously.

"Ah, no. There was an incident yesterday and Dad told me that maybe I should take a couple of days off while he dealt with it."

Crystal's father owned and ran the biggest casting agency in Hollywood. Crystal had been working there for years.

"What did you do?" I asked.

"Why do you automatically think that it was me that did something?" Crystal said indignantly.

I raised an eyebrow.

"Okay, we had Mia Lee trying out for a part and you know that woman can't act at all."

I nodded. Mia Lee was the up and coming It girl in Hollywood. Her publicist was amazing. This woman had come from nowhere and was now dominating all the magazines, news feeds and social media everywhere. So far she had been in a few movies where the most that was asked of her was to look gorgeous, run without knocking herself out with her breasts, and scream on cue.

"So," I said.

"She kept throwing her boobs in our faces with every movement while trying to be dramatic and sexy."

"So…" I said slowly. "Isn't that what she does? Everyone loves her regardless of the way she actually acts."

"She was trying out for the part of a nun."

The look on my face must have shown my disbelief.

"Exactly," said Crystal. "That look on your face was my reaction as well, but some moron decided that the woman who is better known for the way her breasts constantly seem to accidentally fall out of her top, was the best option for playing an innocent nun who is martyred for her beliefs, rather than the dramatically trained actress that I had put forward who was perfect."

"You could have just waited and had a quiet word with your father," I said gently.

"I was going to," Crystal said. "But she started rubbing herself up against the guy playing the priest during a confessional scene. You could see him getting excited about it, but he was trying to concentrate on the scene, and the guys with me on the panel were getting turned on and I just couldn't take it anymore."

"What did you do?" I asked.

"I may have stopped the audition and told her if she really needed to rub up against something, there was a stripper bar around the corner where she could make a bit of money."

"Oh Crystal," I said, shaking my head.

"She got a little upset and started accusing me of compromising her artistic integrity, at which stage I may have pointed out that if she thought that was artistic, then the stripper bar was exactly where she belonged. Needless to say, my Dad is now dealing with the petulant fallout from the woman who will no doubt be gracing our screens in the worst movie ever."

"Not that you're bitter," I said.

"Of course I'm bitter," said Crystal. "I see really good actors and actresses that come through my office all the time, really talented, and they get passed over because they don't have a name or a social media presence or the right plastic surgeon."

I nodded sagely, because really, what was there to say? This was the world we were living in.

"If you want to come and help me find Eric's family, you are more than welcome," I said.

"Thanks," said Crystal. "I think I need to get a dose of reality in my life."

Looking down at the dingy steps of the basement gym where Eric used to work, I mused that Crystal was going to get a massive dose of reality here. The basement gym lights were quite bright after the dimness of the stairs. Two musclebound men covered in tattoos looked us up and down as they passed us. Crystal looked at me in surprise. I had to agree with her. This was not the sort of place that I had expected Eric to be working at. I knew the gym that he had been working at when he met Adele. I had attended it on occasion. My friend, Edwin, worked there sometimes in one of his myriad of part time jobs. It was bright and light and had obviously had a new age consultant involved in the way it was set out. This gym was obviously trying hard but it wasn't quite reaching the atmosphere that only an overpaid expert can achieve.

Looking over at the reception area I was surprised to see Travis Cooper leaning against the desk. He was charming a young lady with six pack abs that I would never be able to achieve without giving up on my weakness for chocolate. The idea was simply so ridiculous it was laughable. Travis straightened up as Crystal and I approached.

"Trudie," he said warmly, and I noticed how Miss Six Pack shot me a dark look.

"Did not expect to see you here," I said suspiciously.

Crystal elbowed me in the side and I stopped myself from wincing.

"This is my friend, Crystal Bronstein," I said, trying to discreetly rub the soreness away from my ribs. "Crystal, this is Travis. What brings you here?"

"After seeing you yesterday I thought I'd follow up on Eric and see if I could give you a bit more assistance."

My eyes narrowed suspiciously. My meeting with Travis yesterday had in no way prepared me for the possibility that he was being helpful. Miss Six Pack was obviously getting a little tired of not being the center of attention and chose that moment to interrupt while breathing in deeply. This served the dual purpose of stopping our conversation and also bringing attention to herself, her impressive abs and her gravity defying breasts.

"As I was saying," she said, amazing me with the way she could talk without letting out the breath she had taken in. "Eric didn't really seem to have any friends who worked here, most of his clientele were women."

"Of course they were," muttered Crystal.

"Then one day he came in and quit. He said he'd hit the jackpot and he'd never have to work again. I never saw him after that day."

Travis looked at me knowingly. Of course, Eric hitting the jackpot would have to be his marriage to Adele. Score one for the romantic cynics of the world.

"Did anyone come looking for him here after he left?" asked Travis.

"No, I mean other than the female clients acting like their lives were over, until they found the next trainer willing to give them that bit of extra encouragement."

Travis smiled and I could see Miss Six Pack falling deeper under his spell. "Any chance of me having a look at his personnel file?"

"I don't know," she said, looking around nervously.

"Eric has died." I tried to look as sympathetic as possible. "We're trying to find out whether he has any family to notify."

She still hesitated.

"His funeral is tomorrow," I said. "I would hate it if his family couldn't be there. They deserve a chance to say goodbye."

I could see her relenting. "I'll be right back," she said, turning to go to the back room.

Travis looked at me expectantly.

"So," I said. "What's the real reason that you are here?"

"Can't I just be trying to help out," he asked, his hands stretched out wide trying to look innocent.

"I've known you for less than twenty-four hours and so far I kind of get the idea that you don't just try to help out for anything. There has to be another angle here."

"Fine then," Travis said, dropping his arms. "There was always something about this guy that bothered me from the start. When Adele married him I dropped it because she told me to, and frankly, I'm a bit too busy to worry about starry eyed romantics with less sense than a sheep." He looked at me meaningfully and I rolled my eyes. "When you came to see me yesterday, I started to get a little concerned that you might walk into whatever situation that was bothering me back then. I had a free couple of hours, so I thought that I would put a few niggling issues to bed before you stepped into it up to your neck."

"You know, for a second there I thought you were doing something to be nice," I said. "Then I remembered who I was speaking to."

Travis grinned just as Miss Six Pack came back with the file and handed it to him.

"Thanks, Sharli," he said.

Of course, her name was Sharli. He quickly looked through the file and then just as I went to lean over and have a look myself he slammed it shut and passed it back to Sharli.

"Thanks for all your help," he said as he grabbed both my and Crystal's elbows and started herding us towards the door.

"Wait a second." Sharli tucked a card in Travis's front pocket. "In case you decide to join I'd be happy to help you out."

"First person I'll call," he said as he almost dragged the two of us out.

Once we were outside and near his car, I wrenched my arm away from him and glared.

"What was that about?"

"I got the information I needed. There was no reason to stick around and you may have the entire day to waste on this but I don't," Travis said patiently as if talking to a child.

"I wasn't asking you to waste any time on this," I said, getting angrier by the second. "Finding Eric's family is my job, not yours. I don't recall at any time asking for your help."

Travis looked over at Crystal. "She's pretty cute when she's angry isn't she?"

"I wouldn't know," said Crystal. "I've never seen her mad before."

"That makes me special," he said, continuing the conversation as if I wasn't even there.

"That makes you annoying," I said, interrupting him. "Just give me the information you got from the file and you can go about your day and make the world a better place in your own special way."

"That doesn't work for me," said Travis.

"Why doesn't that work for you?" I asked impatiently.

"The address I got off his file is in a part of town that is not the best and I'd feel a little uncomfortable with you going there without me."

"Why do you care?" I snapped, exasperated.

"Got a thing for lost causes and deluded romantics," he said, that innocent smile on his face getting to the point I wanted to slap it off.

With Travis and me glaring at each other, Crystal's phone rang.

"Excuse me," she said as she stepped away to answer it.

Travis and I continued our staring contest.

Travis sighed. "Look, I always felt this job was unfinished."

"Adele pulled you from the job, there was nothing else for you to do," I said.

"Yeah, but I always had this niggling feeling that this situation wasn't going to end well. Never expected it to end in Eric's murder, but it always bothered me. I can't help but think that if I had dug a bit deeper at the time, things might not have spiraled out of control like this."

"Adele married Eric with less thought than she takes to decide what to eat each day," I said. "The woman married him after getting you to check on him but before you had a chance to get any results. Then she refused to hear anything you had to say. None of this is your fault. It's all on Adele, and she has to deal with the situation she created."

"She isn't dealing with it though, is she?" Travis said shrewdly. "She's leaving you to deal with it."

"That's my job," I said wryly. "I get paid to take care of the parts of life that these people are not interested in taking care of themselves."

"Seems like we have something in common," Travis said. "I look into those areas that people don't have the guts or expertise to look into."

I sighed with exasperation. "Just give me the information. You are not obligated to look into this and I sure as hell aren't going to start paying you. It's my job and I don't need your help to do it."

"Actually you are going to need his help," said Crystal,

returning to the group. "I need to get back to the office so you are going to need a ride home and I nominate him," she said, pointing at Travis who was now smiling broadly.

"I thought you were supposed to have some time off, you know, because of your lack of tact when dealing with some clients."

"Yes, I thought so too," said Crystal with a big smile on her face. "But it seems one of my other clients, who is so much more important to the agency than Mia, decided to stand up for me and my artistic integrity when dealing with the acting craft."

"What happened?" I asked.

"The producers now want Bella Hudson instead of Mia and she refused to deal with anyone at the agency but me. She also called Mia a talentless hack online."

Crystal was trying her hardest to appear shocked at the turn of events, but I could see the grin that was just dying to break free.

"It's okay, I'll grab a cab," I said.

"Not happening," said Crystal. "I don't want to risk you getting hurt again. Either you go with tall, dark and packing heat or your day ends now."

I knew that look in Crystal's eyes. There was no way she was going to take no for an answer. She was a small thing but she fought dirty. Regardless of the fact I was quite a bit taller than her I had no doubt at all that she could take me down if she felt it was for my own good. Looking at Travis I could see that he wasn't going to be any help at all.

"I'll stay with him." I knew a no compromise negotiation when I saw it.

"Good," she turned to Travis. "You'll take care of her?" she said.

"Won't let her out of my sight," he murmured.

I wished it sounded less like a threat.

Chapter Fifteen

With Crystal gone I looked up and saw a satisfied smile cross Travis's face.

"I don't know why you are so happy," I said. "You've just written off a large part of your day being unpaid."

"I'll live," said Travis as he ushered me over to another nondescript car.

"Really not one of those guys who telegraphs his insecurities with a fancy car," I said as he held the door open for me.

Travis gave a bark of laughter. "You don't believe in holding back do you?" he said.

"Usually I do," I replied. "You're just special I guess."

There was that smile again as he closed my door and went around to the driver's side of the car.

"So where exactly are we headed to?" I asked.

"We are on our way to see Eric's mother," Travis replied.

"Would she have been told about his death yet?" I asked. The thought of being the one to tell this woman that her son had been murdered was not something that I was looking forward to.

"Probably not," Travis said.

My heart sank. I was definitely not the person who should be doing things like this. All of a sudden I was glad that Travis was with me.

"From what I heard, Eric had broken all contact with his mother years ago. The only place her name came up was in that file under next of kin. I was never able to see the file before because Adele pulled the plug and I had other cases to deal with. What I heard about his mother from a couple of the people who knew him made me feel sorry for the guy though."

"That bad?"

"Worse."

"Wonderful," I said, slouching in my seat.

Travis reached over and patted my knee. "Don't worry, I will be right there with you. We'll be a team."

"Great," I grumbled. "That makes me feel so much better."

Pulling up to a house, I looked over at Travis. "Are you sure somebody lives here?" I asked, surprised. The yard was overgrown, with car parts littered around the front garden. The house looked like it was close to being condemned. Paint was peeling off the walls and there were pieces of siding that were broken and hanging precariously.

"Yep, this is where Annie Davis lives. She was eighteen when she had Eric and from what I've been told he had a miserable childhood. Keep close to me at all times. Do not go anywhere on your own."

"Do you think she's dangerous?" I asked.

"I don't know. What I do know is that this area is rife with drugs. There is no pride shown in this house which tells me she is either into drugs, crazy or given up. Or she could be all three."

As we headed up to the front door I could see Travis scanning the area, his body felt tense beside me. I really felt like running, but stiffened my shoulders and followed Travis to the front door. After trying the bell and finding it didn't work Travis knocked on the door. Hearing no movement inside, he knocked again much harder. I stumbled back as the door was ripped open violently and Travis seemed to automatically step in front of me.

"What the hell do you want?" snarled the woman who had answered the door.

"We are looking for Annie Davis," Travis said smoothly.

"You found her, now I'm asking once again, what the hell do you want?"

"Ms Davis," I said, peeking around Travis's shoulder. "My name is Trudie Eyre, I knew your son."

"What's that worthless piece of garbage done this time?" she snarled.

My hopes that she had been told about her son's death plummeted. Trying desperately to find the right words I took in a deep breath to deliver the news but was interrupted by Travis.

"I'm sorry to have to inform you that your son has died."

"Eric's dead?" She appeared stunned but then I could see a cunning look in her eyes replacing the surprise. "So what did he leave me?" she asked. "I mean he was married to that rich bitch which means he has heaps of money. I'm his only family so everything he has comes to me. I know my rights. I gave that boy a home and what did he give me? Nothing. He owes me and I'm going to make sure I get everything that I'm owed."

By this time her eyes were becoming unfocused and I could see that she was going into crazy land. I noticed Travis's hand on my forearm, warning me not to provoke the woman. I realized that she was coming unhinged but the stupid part of me was not going to be silenced.

"Ms Davis, Eric's funeral is going to be tomorrow. Would you like a chance to say goodbye to him?" I asked, trying to ignore the incredulous look I was getting from Travis.

I know, it was a stupid question, but there was a part of me that kept thinking this was Eric's mother. Surely there had to be some small part of the maternal instinct in her. I couldn't imagine anyone who had given birth and raised a child not wanting to have that final chance to say goodbye.

"If he hasn't left me anything I hope he burns in hell where he belongs," she spat out and slammed the door.

I stared at the scarred door stunned by the turn of events.

"Well, you have your answer" said Travis cheerfully as

he started making his way down the steps off the front porch. "Looks like our work here is done."

I followed him numbly. I never thought that I would get to a point in my life when I would feel the need to give Eric Wesson a hug, but I had to say I had reached that point. I shuddered to think what Eric's childhood had been like. Tears pricked the back of my eyelids when I realized that the poor kid had never stood a chance.

"You okay?" Travis asked, compassion in his voice.

"Just making sure I call my mom tonight. I'm suddenly feeling the need to thank her for actually being my mom. Right at this moment I'm kind of feeling like I won the lottery when it comes to her."

"Yeah, it's times like these that you wish some people had to take a test or something before they breed."

"Scary thing is that I am kind of agreeing with you," I said, smiling up at him.

"Can't have that happening," said Travis, smiling back.

Suddenly I heard a crash behind us and Annie Davis came charging out of the house with a baseball bat waving around above her head.

"You're keeping his money aren't you," she screamed. "It belongs to me, you have to give it to me. I won't let you take what is mine."

As she came towards us with the bat weaving drunkenly in our direction, Travis grabbed me and pushed me hurriedly towards the car. At the last moment he pulled me away as she swung the bat and it connected with the passenger door. The second hit smashed the windscreen. She was screaming obscenities at us as Travis calmly watched her destroying his car while he pulled out his cell phone, all the time keeping a close eye on the woman who was completely redecorating his ride.

"What are you doing?" I asked, perplexed at his casual stance.

"Calling the cops," he said calmly.

I looked at him incredulously. "Why don't you stop

her?" I said as we both winced as the windscreen finally gave way under the relentless onslaught and caved inwards.

"I'm not taking care of it because the only weapon I'm carrying is a gun. Police have all these non-lethal toys and negotiators who can deal with nutjobs like this, but if you're keen for me to shoot her, I can do that if it would make you happier."

I looked at him sourly. "You know, I'm glad it's your car she's doing that to because I kind of think that you have done many things to deserve this kind of karma. You seem to be taking it a lot better than I would have thought you would."

"It's just a clunker I use for work. This kind of thing happens to my cars, so I only use those for work that it doesn't hurt me to see destroyed."

"This kind of thing happens to you a lot?" I asked, deciding that maybe he had the right idea and I should just sit back and watch Annie destroy the car. Now that I had realized she wasn't going to attack us and was content to take her frustration out on the car, I was able to relax and enjoy the show.

"Relatively regularly," he said, pulling out some gum and offering me a stick. I refused and he shrugged and popped one into his mouth. "Most times when you catch people cheating they have a tendency to take that personally. With the clientele I work for, we are talking massive amounts of money. That tends to bring out the inner caveman in many people. Wish I could say this is the first time someone's taken to my car with a baseball bat. In fact it's probably about the sixth or seventh time."

"You live a very strange life," I said.

"Maybe, but I get paid very well for it. Ahh, here come our heroes to save the day," Travis said sarcastically.

Sure enough a squad car came screeching around the corner and a couple of uniformed officers jumped out, screaming at Annie to drop the baseball bat. She froze in midswing, spun around and fixed Travis with a glare.

"You called the cops," she accused.

I was kind of glad that she was placing the blame firmly where she should have, right up until the point she started advancing towards us, still swinging that bat above her head. I was beginning to be impressed by her stamina. The woman had been swinging that thing for a good ten minutes and she didn't even seem to be particularly winded. Travis pulled me backwards as Annie was coming towards us. The police were yelling at her to put down the bat. We seemed to be in some weird dance where for every step Annie took forward, Travis and I moved backwards. Luckily one of the cops finally realized that the woman was not going to give up until she started using Travis, and unfortunately by default me, as the man would not let go of my arm, as a piñata. He also decided, for whatever reason, that she didn't deserve lethal force and so unloaded a stun gun into her. Down she went to the ground with a slightly surprised look on her face, as if she never imagined this was going to happen to her.

As the police surrounded her and kicked away the baseball bat I started to relax but almost jumped out of my skin when a quiet voice came from behind me. "What's happened to Annie?"

Behind me I found a young woman peering over the fence from Annie's neighbor's house.

"Annie took exception to some news we had to tell her," I said, surprised that I was still able to speak calmly as I watched Travis inspect the mangled wreckage that until fifteen minutes ago had been his car.

"Is Eric okay?" the woman asked anxiously as she came through a gate in the fence.

"Why do you assume it is about Eric?" I asked curiously.

"She blames Eric for everything that is wrong with her life." The woman shrugged. "According to Annie she was going to conquer the world right up until the moment that she got pregnant with Eric, which of course was his fault.

Everything bad that has happened since then, was on him. So what did he do this time to set her off?"

There it was again, that insane urge to hug the man. The more I heard about Eric's life, the more I felt sorry for him.

"He died," I answered without thinking and immediately wanted to kick myself when I saw the devastation that one little sentence had caused. I grabbed her arm as she looked like she was going to faint. "I'm sorry. I shouldn't have said it like that," I said as I helped lower her to the curb. "Here, put your head between your knees. Did you know him?"

"I grew up next door," she mumbled, keeping her head down, not looking at me.

"My name is Trudie," I said. "I work for Eric's wife. The funeral is tomorrow if you want to be there."

I looked over to see that Annie had started to recover from being stunned and was now swearing loudly and with great creativity at the poor young cop who looked like he was regretting his choice regarding the use of non-lethal force.

Travis seemed to be chatting away with the older officer, and from the looks of him he was not perturbed at the events that had occurred. Meanwhile I was sitting in the street rubbing circles on the back of some woman I didn't know.

"What's your name?" I asked gently because at this point I had nothing else to say.

"Ruby," she said, sniffing quietly.

"I'm really sorry, Ruby," I said. The poor woman looked devastated. For the first time I was actually seeing real grief from someone with regards to Eric's death.

Travis walked over to us.

"Trudie, the cops need to get your statement."

I looked at Ruby, feeling torn. She wiped her eyes and gave me a watery smile.

"I'm fine, it's just a bit of a shock. I've known Eric all

my life."

"Do you know if Eric had any other family other than his mother?" I asked.

"No, it was just Annie and Eric. His dad was never in the picture and according to Annie having Eric was the worst thing that had ever happened to her, so she made sure that she was never able to have any more kids."

I nodded sympathetically, unsure how to respond to such a callous statement. After giving her the details for the funeral I watched as she walked back to her house.

"Poor kid," Travis murmured.

"Yeah," I said distractedly.

"Officer Eldridge needs to take your statement," Travis said. "So I can get the ball rolling on insurance for the car."

I looked at him with some astonishment. "You've got insurance on that thing?"

"Course I do. My mama always said you should never get on the road without insurance."

"You've got a mother?" I said, the surprise evident in my voice.

"Of course I do," Travis said. "How do you think I got here?"

"Never really considered it," I replied. "Though if I had to think about it, the process probably includes dark magic and the utter hopelessness of the human condition."

Travis looked at me sourly. "Nice," he said. "If I was any less sure of my place in the world I would be hurt by that."

"Good to know," I replied.

"Ma'am," the officer interrupted. "Can you tell me what happened?"

"We came to see Annie Davis and tell her about her son's funeral and see if she wanted to attend. She said she didn't and slammed the door on us. We went to leave and she came racing out of the house with a baseball bat, waving it over her head and then started attacking the car."

"At any time did you feel she was targeting you?"

"At first I was a bit concerned she might come after us, but Travis pulled me out of the way and after that she just seemed focused on turning the car into a piece of scrap metal."

"Seems she succeeded," the officer murmured.

"To be perfectly honest it didn't look much better before she started her redecorating project," I said.

Eldridge chuckled. Once the officer was finished I walked over to where Travis was taking photos of the car with his phone.

"Getting proof for the insurance company?" I asked.

"That and the wall of fame," he said. He could obviously see the questioning look on my face. "These old cars are often punished for my work so we have a wall of the results."

"You live in a very strange world," I said.

Travis grinned. "But I'm very rarely bored."

"You're enjoying this," I said accusingly.

"Why yes, I believe I am," he said. "And I think my day is just going to become more fun." I followed the direction of his eyes to see Griffin getting out of the car he had just pulled up in.

"Don't aggravate him," I warned.

"Oh, honey, you're just trying to take away all of my fun."

"You do realize that you have a demented sense of fun," I said.

"Never said I didn't," Travis grinned.

I rolled my eyes. Griffin was looking over at us as he was talking to one of the officers and I could tell that he was not happy. Whether this was because I had once again found myself in a volatile situation, or the fact that Travis seemed to feel very comfortable in my company, I couldn't really tell.

"He does not look happy," said Travis, keeping a smile on his face as he looked over at Griffin.

"I don't know why he is even here," I mumbled. "I mean it's not like there is a dead body anywhere around here."

"Oh, I think this has a bit more to do with the fact that you are here, or he may have heard that I'm involved. Either of those situations is pretty much guaranteed to pique his interest," Travis said as Griffin walked towards us.

"Cooper," Griffin said, his eyes on me.

"Griffin," Travis replied with the same level of gravity in his voice.

I looked at him sharply and his eyes were still sparkling with mischief.

"Time to go home, Trudie," Griffin said, finally addressing me.

"Travis is going to need a lift home as well," I said, ignoring the look of censure on Griffin's face.

There was silence for a second before Travis broke it. "Thanks for the offer, Trudie, but I need to sort out the towing for my car."

"Are you sure?" I asked and by this stage I didn't know whether I meant it or whether I was just putting off being in the same car with Griffin. I could see a muscle ticking in his jaw and frankly I wasn't too keen to be alone with him when he let loose.

"Don't you worry your pretty little head about me," said Travis.

I rolled my eyes and couldn't help the exasperated sigh that escaped. Griffin stiffened and I stifled the impulse to throw something at Travis.

"I'll organize a new ride and give you a call later." He grinned and I knew he was getting way too much satisfaction in needling Griffin.

Chapter Sixteen

Sitting in the car with Griffin I started to wish that I had stayed with Travis. The tension in the car was thick and as he didn't start talking I wasn't really inclined to break the silence, which made for a wonderful ride home. When we got to the carpark of the apartment complex I quickly jumped out of the car.

"Thanks for the ride, I'll see you later," I said and quickly started heading for my apartment.

I heard Griffin grunt behind me and follow me up to my door. I didn't think I was going to get away with it. Once inside I dropped my bag on the table, turned around and braced myself for the interrogation. Silence. What the hell was I supposed to do with that? I crossed my arms.

"Okay, you're obviously upset about something, but it's not up to me to try to deep read your psyche, so either tell me why your panties are in a bunch or get the hell out of my home."

Griffin arched an eyebrow. "Panties in a bunch?" he queried, a slight smile playing around his lips.

"Yes," I said, pointing a finger at him. "I don't even know why you were there, I mean there weren't any bodies. There wasn't even much of a crime. According to Travis that kind of thing happens to him all the time."

"How about the fact that you were in a volatile situation that could have turned nasty at any time, with a person who I personally would not trust your safety to."

"I was perfectly safe with Travis," I said as I flopped down on the couch. "The guy wasn't going to let anything happen to me."

"Why?" asked Griffin.

"Why what?" I replied.

"Why are you so sure that Cooper would keep you safe?"

"I don't know," I said. "Despite what I would call some questionable life choices, the guy seems to be very protective and he was pretty determined to keep me out of a dangerous situation today."

"What were you doing at Annie Davis's house?" Griffin asked, back to business again.

"The funeral is being held tomorrow," I said. "My job includes finding any family that Eric had and seeing if they wanted to go to the funeral."

"And you naturally assumed that Annie Davis would want to go to her son's funeral," Griffin said, sighing.

"You knew she was Eric's mother," I said.

"Of course we knew, it came up in the investigation. To be perfectly honest I was going out to speak to her when Ramos called me to let me know that you were a possible assault victim at the Davis house."

"Not me, just the car," I said.

"Yeah, well, sometimes the information that comes through on first reports can be a little inaccurate," Griffin said wryly, and I got a glimpse of the worry he had gone through in the tightness around his eyes.

"The only time I was worried was when she came charging out with the bat and Travis pulled me out of the way," I said. "After that she was so busy beating up Travis's car that I think she kind of forgot about us and we were left to watch. It ended up being more of a spectator sport than an actual crime."

"And Cooper just let it happen?" questioned Griffin.

"Well yes," I said. "I asked him if he was going to do anything to stop her from destroying his car and he said his only option was to shoot her. Said it would be better if we waited for the cops to come up with non-lethal force, which they did. Stun gun took her down easy."

"The Travis Cooper I remember wouldn't have been quite so patient with the situation," Griffin said as he shrugged out of his jacket and sat on the couch.

Bemused at the way he was making himself comfortable in my home I was surprised with what he had said. "Really, because Travis seems pretty laid back to me. I can't see him getting heated up about anything. Seriously if he was wound tight I would have thought he'd go completely nuts over the way that car was destroyed."

"Maybe he's changed over the last couple of years."

"Ever planning on telling me about what the problem is between the two of you?" I asked, sitting down next to him. He started tucking my hair behind my ear and playing with the strands, twirling them around his finger.

"It's all ancient history. I just don't like the idea of you being around him. He has a tendency to attract trouble. Take today for example."

"To be fair," I said. "He only came along to make sure that I was safe. It is probably better that he was there because if that car hadn't been there to take up her attention, she may have decided to use that bat on me."

"I still don't like the fact that he seems to have taken an interest in you," Griffin sighed. "Look, I don't want to get into it but my relationship with Cooper is kind of complicated. I would hate to think he was using you to get under my skin."

I sat up straight. "Do you really think that he would do that?"

"Honestly, there was a time when I wouldn't have thought that at all, but things happened that made me start thinking that I didn't know the guy as well as I thought I did. I don't want you to have anything to do with him," he said abruptly.

I drew back, surprised at the quick change of subject.

"You are kidding aren't you, please tell me that you are not stupid enough to tell me who I can and can't work with."

"I'm just saying that Travis Cooper is not the sort of person that I want anywhere near you. You could have got hurt today."

"Correction," I said angrily, "I could have got hurt if Travis hadn't been there. He took care of me. On my own I'd have probably walked into that baseball bat."

"Oh that just fills me with confidence," Griffin said sarcastically. "You have to think before you get yourself into these situations. I am getting tired of being called to a scene and finding you in the middle of it."

"I am doing my job. I'm sorry if that concerns you but I really don't think that you have any say in what I do," I said angrily.

At that moment my cell phone rang. Snatching it up I barked into it. "What?"

There was silence and then I heard Adele's voice on the line.

"Trudie, is that you?"

I immediately softened my tone. "Adele, I'm so sorry. I was distracted elsewhere."

I glared as Griffin grabbed his jacket and angrily shoved his arms into it.

"Trudie, did Miranda speak to you yesterday?"

"Miranda spoke to me a couple of times, was there anything in particular that you are referring to?" I queried.

"There were some photos that I wanted you to get for me."

"The photos in the safe in your closet," I recalled. "Oh yes, Miranda told me about them yesterday. With all the funeral planning I haven't had a chance to get back to the house. In fact, I can't see myself getting back there today. Do you need them immediately or would it be okay for me to get them out of the safe tomorrow after the funeral?"

"I guess I don't need to get them right now but I would like them as soon as you can get to the house," Adele said.

"If they're important I may be able to get them today."

"No," said Adele. "I guess it doesn't matter anymore, Miranda is just encouraging me to work, to help with the trauma."

"Okay," I said, a bit mystified by the tone in her voice. "Was there anything else you needed?"

"Everything is taken care of for tomorrow?" she asked quietly.

"It will be, I'm just organizing some final details."

"Did you find any of Eric's family?" she asked.

"Yes," I said hesitantly. "I found his mother. Unfortunately I don't think she will be able to attend the funeral."

"Oh well, I'm sure you did your best."

I had to actually control myself from sighing out loud. It would be useless to inform Adele that her little errand for me ended up with a baseball bat being waved around and a car being destroyed. The woman truly lived in her own world. I was beginning to find myself becoming impatient with her. It was an unfortunate side effect of my business that you learned a little too much about people you were impressed with from afar. I loved Adele's books but I have to say that I was getting a little tired of the constant neediness. There was silence.

"Was there anything else that you needed?" I prompted gently.

"No, nothing at all," she said and yet again I wondered what sort of medication she was currently on.

"Adele," I said after waiting a couple more seconds for her to continue talking. "I think you should have a lie down, maybe get some sleep before tomorrow. It's going to be a draining day."

"You're right of course," said Adele. "What would I do without you? Although Miranda's here, she'll help me."

I muttered a prayer of gratitude.

"Could you put Miranda on the phone please, Adele?"

Without answering, the phone was passed over.

"Trudie, is that you?" I heard Miranda's voice.

"Yes it is, is Adele okay?" I asked.

"I think she is under a lot of strain at the moment," Miranda said in that cool voice of hers. "I think once we've got through tomorrow she can begin healing from this traumatic event."

Getting off the phone I had to agree with Miranda. Adele had never struck me as a particularly strong person. It seemed that Eric's death was only serving to highlight her need to rely on those people around her. Turning around I found Griffin with a serious look on his face.

"I think I need to go," he said. "It looks like you are going to be busy for the rest of the day."

"Probably a good idea," I agreed.

Griffin took a step toward me and then stopped as if unsure as to how he should proceed.

"I don't want you to get hurt," he said softly.

"Don't try to give me orders," I said. "Trust me when I tell you that will not end well."

Griffin nodded and started heading for the door. I followed him and he stopped abruptly and turned around.

"Please promise me that you'll try not to put yourself in any danger."

I nodded. That was an easy promise to make. I always tried to keep myself out of danger. Unfortunately it seemed that no matter how hard I tried, I ended up in dangerous situations.

His head ducked as he kissed me. The kiss was sweet and gentle, so totally at odds with the domineering attitude he had been using on me, and my eyes fluttered closed. His strong arms pulled me against him and I felt my head spin as the passion was rising in me. All I could think was I wanted to get closer. Pulling away from me he smiled as he looked down into my flushed features.

"That is what I want," Griffin said softly as his thumb stroked my cheek. "I want you looking at me like that, every day."

With that he walked out the door. I closed it and leaning my back against it, I sank to the floor, trying desperately to control the raging fantasies going through my head. Jake Griffin may annoy the hell out of me sometimes, but man could he kiss.

Chapter Seventeen

Standing in the foyer of the funeral home waiting for Tomas, I tried desperately to rein those fantasies in as I contemplated the floral arrangements dotted around the room. The colors were a light pastel cream which looked a lot more tasteful than I would have expected. In fact I had to give Tomas points for the entire place. It was out of the way and looked like a small stately home on acreage at the end of a long driveway. There had even been a security guard at the gate to the property. I don't think we would have been able to find a more discreet place to hold the funeral. Bustling in, Tomas came up to me and hugged me, kissing me on the cheek.

"Trudie, I'm so sorry to keep you waiting."

"That's okay," I said. "Where did you find this place? It is absolutely perfect."

"You wouldn't believe the places that are around for funerals," Tomas said. He grabbed my hand. "Now I need you to have a look at Eric to make sure that he is acceptable for the viewing tomorrow."

I stopped short and Tomas who had my hand and was obviously lighter than me got yanked back.

"Nuh uh," I said, shaking my head. "I am not looking at a dead body."

Tomas looked at me patiently, "Sweetie," he said, using that calming voice which really just has a tendency to put me on edge. "Weren't you the one who found the body?"

I nodded.

"In that case you've already seen the man dead."

"Yes I have, and that image is one that I would be very happy if I could remove it from my brain. I really do not need to have a reinforcement with several days of decomposition added on top."

"Oh, honey," Tomas said, grabbing my hand again and dragging me forward. For a little guy he sure had some strength to him when he got going.

"Trust me, Helena is a genius. You won't believe what she has managed to do."

He dragged me through the building, pointing out flowers and colors, accepting my murmurs as approval until we got to the morgue. As Tomas opened the door I stopped breathing through my nose, expecting a horrendous smell, but was instead greeted with a mixture of herbal scents. Underneath you could still smell the sharp antiseptic odor that I would have anticipated. Covering it was a riot of different aromas, seemingly fighting each other for dominance. Walking into the morgue it looked like I had stepped into a greenhouse. There were plants all over the room. In the middle of the room was a table with a body on it and standing over him was a woman wearing a long flowing dress, her platinum blonde hair cascading down her back. There were a multitude of bracelets running up her arms that clinked together with every movement she made. She looked ethereal, like the ultimate hippy child. I will admit that when Tomas had said the name Helena I had been expecting someone Goth-like and sullen. The look on Helena's face was one of unmitigated joy and it looked completely out of place in a funeral home. I hung back as Helena and Tomas air kissed each other without actually touching. Tomas waved me forward.

"Helena, this is Trudie. She was a friend of Eric and she just wanted to thank you for doing such an amazing job with him."

I stepped forward and was immediately engulfed with the scent of citrus and lavender.

"I should be thanking you," she gushed. "Eric has been so wonderful to work with. His spirit is so calming. I could see he was a beautiful soul. You must miss him dreadfully."

I thought that missing him may have been an overstatement and I was distracted by how friendly Helena was being. She continued her talking, all the time stroking my hair.

"He is so beautiful. It was an honor to work on him, like working on a Van Gogh."

I looked at Tomas, a little confused. Sure, Eric had been gorgeous in life, I wasn't going to deny that for a second. That being said, despite my albeit brief glance at Eric on the morning he died, I was pretty sure that beautiful did not exactly cover how he looked after death. I had also recommended a closed casket, because I didn't think Adele would be able to cope with what had happened to Eric, and the aftermath. Helena pointed to the table and I got my first glimpse of Eric.

"Holy cow," I blurted out, because the Eric lying on the table was not the one I saw in the bed three days ago.

I didn't think that I had been traumatized that much, but my memories of that morning had blood matting his hair and too much damage to ever be seen again. Combined with the autopsy, I was sure there would be no way he would have been presentable for an open casket. This Eric looked like he had been sleeping and would get up at any moment. He had barely looked this healthy when he was alive. I looked dumbfounded at Helena and Tomas.

"He looks amazing," I said.

Helena jumped up and down and clapped her hands. She then gave me a quick hug and rushed out of the room.

I looked at Tomas. "Seriously, is this really him or is it one of those wax dummies?"

Tomas nodded. "It's him. I'm telling you, Helena is a genius. I have brought her some really bad ones before and she seems to be able to fix them up." He coughed. "She is a little eccentric so we don't usually let her speak to the families, but she is a real artist. I mean, you should have seen the size of the hole in the side of his head."

"What do you mean, hole?" I asked.

"From the bullet."

"Eric was shot?" I asked.

"Yes, went in the right temple with a nice little hole, came out the left side with a hole the size of a golf ball. You didn't know he was shot?"

"No, I was only in the room for a few minutes when I found the body. All I saw was a lot of blood on the pillow. Why would someone shoot him but leave Adele alive?"

"Maybe Adele did it," Tomas offered.

"And then went to bed and fell asleep beside the dead body of her husband," I said doubtfully. "I can't see many people doing that, and I have to say that I really don't believe that Adele could be that callous or crazy."

Looking at Eric, I was simply amazed that he looked so good. "Where exactly was he shot?" I asked Tomas.

Tomas looked at the head. "The bullet went in here," he said as he pointed to the right temple. "And it looks like the bullet came out here."

"How can you tell?" I asked, looking at where he was pointing.

"If you look really closely you can see where Helena has grafted on some hair from other parts of his head."

I looked closely. No, I couldn't see it. Helena was truly gifted, but I would take Tomas's word for it. Helena bustled back in the room.

"You have negative energy around you," she said as she waved a burning incense stick in my direction.

I looked at Tomas in panic. I'll admit the woman was an artist but she was beginning to worry me. Tomas stepped in front of me and cut Helena off as she started chanting.

"Trudie is fine, Helena," he said.

Helena kept chanting and waving the smoking stick at me. It wasn't a small stick either. This thing looked more like a tree branch with greenery tied to the end of it. This greenery was on fire and was putting out a lot of smoke. I could feel my eyes beginning to water. As I breathed in I started coughing as the smoke went into my lungs. An alarm started blaring loudly and another man came running into the room.

"For God's sake, Helena," he yelled as he grabbed the burning stick and doused it in the nearest sink. "I've told you, no burning things in this room."

He pulled out a small step ladder and turned off the smoke alarm. Helena stamped her foot and pouted.

"I hate you," she said, before storming off.

"Tomas, why do you let her do things like that?" the newcomer said.

"Don't blame me, Rico," Tomas said. "I was trying to stop her. I thought you'd taken away anything that she could use to light a fire after the last incident."

"I did," Rico said morosely, "but it's a full time job trying to keep her from doing her earth witch thing."

Rico turned his attention to me. "I'm sorry about that."

"Not a problem," I said, tears streaming down my face. I gratefully accepted the tissue Tomas passed to me and started to wipe the tears away. "I think she was trying to help me with some negative energy that I have."

"Do you really have negative energy?" Rico asked.

"Well in the last few months I've stumbled over a couple of dead bodies and I've been shot. I'm guessing Helena was pretty much spot on about the negative energy. Thinking about it, you may have stopped her a bit early. I think I may need her to start up again, maybe with a burning tree trunk."

"Fine," said Rico. "But next time do it in your house. Hopefully there'd be a few less ignition sources in there."

I looked around and noticed the bottles of chemicals dotted around the room, mostly obscured by the plant life that seemed to have taken over the area.

"Getting your point," I said, still dabbing at my eyes. Turning to Tomas I asked, "Is there anything else that I need to do for tomorrow?"

"No," said Tomas. "The viewing will happen first, the

service straight after. As it is only a small function we have tea and coffee and some food in the reception room after the funeral. That should be everything."

"Thank you so much," I said. "You have no idea how much this has helped."

"Oh, by the way," said Tomas. "Did you manage to find any family that I need to talk to regarding any special requests?"

"Ah yes," I said, looking at Tomas and Rico. "His mother won't be attending the funeral and doesn't really have much of an interest in anything happening with it."

"Any reason?" asked Tomas.

"Other than her being the mother from hell, chances are she will still be in jail tomorrow."

"In jail?" Tomas queried.

"Yes, she didn't take the news of Eric's death and not leaving her anything too well. Decided to take it out on a friend's car with a baseball bat. I'm pretty sure he decided to press charges."

Tomas and Rico looked at me in shock. Tomas recovered first.

"Very well, in that case we go with standard service, no frills, I'll pass the information you gave me on to the funeral celebrant and we should get it done easily."

I felt a little bad that I was looking at Eric's funeral as something that I needed to get through with as little effort as possible. It seemed wrong to me, but there wasn't much I could do about it. I had tried to find someone who would truly mourn for Eric but he obviously hadn't led the kind of life which provided for that. I kept telling myself that it wasn't my fault but there was still a part of me that felt guilty.

Chapter Eighteen

Sitting on my couch later in the evening that guilt was still eating at me. My cell rang and I picked it up.

"Hey, Trudie," Griffin said.

I smiled. "Hi, Griffin."

"I just wanted to see what you were doing this evening."

"Just sitting on the couch trying to find a show that doesn't have me cringing at what people are willing to do for their fifteen minutes of fame."

"Not a fan of reality television?" Griffin asked.

"Not even close."

"Thought you might be working at Adele's house."

"No, not tonight. I've got to go pick up something for Adele but I think I'll do it tomorrow after the funeral."

"That's good," Griffin said. "I was hoping to come over and see you tonight but I've got work so I may see you tomorrow."

"Okay," I said. "I'll see you then. Be careful."

"Thanks," said Griffin. "Sleep well. Wish I was with you."

He hung up and I smiled. I had to admit it, I was enjoying this, whatever it was, with Griffin. I couldn't really categorize it as a relationship, but it was something. It was definitely something.

The next morning the sun was shining brightly as it usually does in LA. Arriving at the funeral home early, I found Tomas rushing around organizing things.

"Is everything okay?" I asked as I grabbed the massive vase of flowers that he was trying to balance on top of a pile of paperwork.

"Everything is fine," he said, nodding to Rico as he

raced past us.

"Are you sure?" I said. "You both look a little tense."

"Tense?" queried Tomas.

"Yes, tense is the word that I'm going for," I said, smiling.

"If you must know we're not tense." He glared at me. "Helena decided that the funeral we had planned today was not good enough for Eric and that his spirit wasn't at peace. She decided to perform a séance last night to try to talk to him. She kind of made a bit of a mess but we are dealing with it."

Inwardly I groaned. Even dead, women were falling for Eric and making my life difficult.

"What do you need me to do?" I said, following Tomas into the room where Eric was now peacefully laid out in a coffin. Next to him was a chalked circle on the floor with all kinds of symbols written on it and melted wax candles.

"What was she trying to do?" I groaned.

"How the hell should I know?" Tomas growled, obviously past the time when he should have had his morning coffee. "She thinks his spirit is not at rest for some reason."

"Maybe the fact he was murdered," I ventured as I got down on my knees to try to scrape some of the melted wax off the floor."

"She keeps going on about him having a beautiful spirit."

I wondered if she meant that metaphorically. The Eric I knew had a beautiful body. Spirit though, that was a little less attractive. I reached into my bag and found the small Swiss Army knife my brother had given me when I left home. I pulled out the blade to start scraping the worst of the wax off the floor. Tomas looked at me dumbfounded.

"What?" I asked.

"You have a knife in your bag," he said quietly.

"I have a Swiss Army knife. It is a tool. See, it even has tweezers," I said, pulling out the tiny tweezers and waving them around.

"In case you have a hair plucking emergency," Tomas ventured.

"In my line of work you would be amazed at what I am required to do at times," I grumbled. "For example, at times I am required to be on my hands and knees next to the coffin of my employer's murdered husband, while scraping the candle wax off the wood floor from the séance performed by the funeral cosmetologist, who has developed a somewhat disturbing attachment to the dead husband."

Tomas stared. "Point taken," he said as he went back to washing away the chalk marks on the floor.

Rico walked in. "I am going to fire her," he growled.

"No you're not," said Tomas.

"What if the family finds out?"

"I've met the family and frankly as long as Helena was able to get some bank account details out of him they'd be cheering her on," I said, still concentrating on the wax.

Rico's exasperation at the situation was obvious to both Tomas and myself. He sat down heavily on the ground just watching Tomas and me as we continued to clean the floor.

"I don't know what to do with her," he said quietly. "I promised our parents I'd take care of her, but if she starts destroying the business I'm going to have to do something."

Tomas leaned over and put his arm around Rico's shoulder.

"We can deal with that later. For now, we clean up and get this funeral done to the best of our ability. She didn't do anything illegal, just thoughtless. That's fine, thoughtless we can deal with. Trudie's here and she is going to help us."

I nodded encouragingly as I kept working.

"We can pull this off, Rico, we just need to work together." Tomas squeezed Rico's shoulder encouragingly and I could see Rico's resolve strengthen.

"Thanks," he said. "And thank you, Trudie. You shouldn't have to do this."

I waved. "Not a problem, we'll have this sorted in no time. One question though, where is Helena now?"

"My aunt is taking care of her for me. She was pretty tired out after last night," he gestured to the mess around us.

Tomas and I went back to work while Rico continued rushing around. Within a half hour we had managed to clean away the chalk residue, candle wax and some substances which I didn't look at too closely, until the original deep brown floorboards shone through. Putting out the chairs I was surprised to see Griffin in the doorway, dressed in a dark suit that highlighted the breadth of his shoulders. In that moment I decided that as much as I liked Griffin in jeans, I really liked him in a suit. I smiled at him but was surprised when I didn't get an answering smile back.

"What are you doing here?" he blurted out.

"I'm working," I said shortly, a little confused by his greeting. Admittedly I hadn't been expecting him to sweep me into his arms and give me a passionate kiss, especially with Eric's corpse lying only meters away. But I had hoped we'd progressed to a much better greeting than that.

"It's just that the funeral doesn't start for another hour," he said. "I expected you to be helping with preparing Adele."

"Miranda and Elliot Powell are taking care of Adele. My job was to organize the funeral and I just came to help Tomas and Rico."

"Oh," Griffin said.

"Now that we've established why I'm here," I said slowly. "Why are you here?"

"Cops always attend the funeral," Griffin said hurriedly. "It is a murder after all."

"You think the murderer will come to the funeral?" I

asked.

"Never know," Griffin said.

We looked at each other in an awkward silence for a second. Tomas poked his head around the door, frowned at the incredibly tense scene before him, and cleared his throat.

"Trudie, could you give me a hand in the reception area. We have a couple of small issues, teeny issues really, and I just need your input."

"Sure," I said slowly.

Tomas looked at Griffin. "Rico doesn't like people walking around before the funeral," he said. You'll have to go."

Griffin looked strangely reluctant to leave.

"Griffin's fine," I said. "He's with me. He won't do anything he shouldn't."

"As long as you're sure," Tomas said.

"Absolutely," I smiled. "He won't touch a thing."

Tomas nodded before heading off.

"You're okay here?" I asked Griffin.

"I'll just have a look around, get a bit or an idea about the place before the funeral starts," Griffin answered.

I nodded and followed Tomas out the door. We almost ran into Griffin's partner, Ramos, who as usual looked like she had just stepped off of a catwalk runway.

"He's in there," I indicated with my head the room we had just left.

"Thanks, Trudie," Ramos smiled as she walked past.

Well at least she was acting normally. Tomas looked at me quizzically.

"What was that all about?"

"I truly don't know," I said. "They're the cops investigating Eric's murder."

"Things seemed a bit tense back there," Tomas ventured. "You and the big cop have something going on?"

"Something," I said distractedly.

Griffin had acted strangely. Unfortunately I had no time to ponder the way he was acting as the next hour saw Tomas, Rico and I working solidly to put this funeral service together. By the time Adele arrived with the Powells, the funeral home looked elegant and subdued. The remnants of Helena's attempts to provide peace to Eric's restless spirit were nowhere to be seen. Neither were Griffin or Ramos for that matter. I hadn't seen them since the awkward interlude in the service room and if I hadn't been so busy I would have been curious to speak to Griffin about what was happening with Eric's case.

Chapter Nineteen

Adele walked into the funeral home with Miranda and Elliot Powell both supporting an arm. She was dressed all in black and looked decidedly frail. When she saw me she let go of Miranda and Elliot and threw her arms around my neck.

"Oh, Trudie, thank you so much for taking care of this for me. You have been a true angel through my time of need."

I didn't say anything, just patted her awkwardly on the back.

"I want to see him," she said as she disentangled herself from me.

"He's just in here," I said, pointing towards the room where Eric's coffin was.

Adele gripped my hand. "Can you come in with me?" she said.

I stopped, looking in the direction of the Powells.

"Surely you'd prefer..."

"No, I want you to come in with me," she insisted.

"Of course," I said as she laid her arm on mine and put a reassuring smile on my face.

Looking down at Eric it hit me again about how precarious life could be.

"He looks just like he's sleeping," Adele murmured as she stroked his face. "I should never have married him. I knew it was a mistake. All I wanted from him was sex. He was great in bed but anytime he started talking I just wanted to tell him to shut up. I couldn't stand to hear him talk. I really shouldn't have married him if I didn't like talking to him should I?"

"Probably not," I said, wondering where else this conversation was going to go.

"You wouldn't marry a man just for sex would you, Trudie?" she asked, all the time stroking Eric's cheek.

For some reason that little movement of her hand was beginning to truly disturb me. I wasn't a fan of Eric but I really didn't think that we needed to spend his funeral dissecting his many, many flaws.

"No, I don't think I would," I said.

"No you wouldn't," Adele said. "I look at you and wish I was that capable. I could never be alone like you. I always needed to have a man taking care of me, ever since I was a girl. Even now, the thought of being alone, I can't do it. I need to have someone. You don't need anyone. You have no one in your life but you are able to cope. I could never live a lonely life like that."

I almost protested that I wasn't lonely but stopped myself. She obviously needed to get this out and it wouldn't be the first time I had acted as therapist to one of my clients.

"I hated him," Adele said and I almost had to hold myself back from pulling her hand away from his face. "He thought he was hurting me by sleeping with all those women. Every time I looked at him, all I felt was disgust and loathing, but I still couldn't stop myself from going to him every night. What does that say about me?" she asked, her eyes filling up with tears."

I grabbed her hand and pulled it away from the stroking motion she had been doing.

"Surely there were some good memories you have of him," I said desperately. "Why don't you try to hold on to those today?"

She looked at me sadly. "I can't," she said. "I hated him so much. This was all for the best." She smiled brightly through her tears. "You'll see, Trudie, this has all been for the best. It was the only way I could get away from him."

She walked out of the room and despite the warm weather I shivered. As soon as this funeral was over, I was going to go home and try my hardest to forget this whole thing had happened. I was then going to think very seriously about my career options. Maybe I could be a dog walker.

Outside the viewing room I could see that several more people had joined the group. Most were friends of Adele's, obviously here to support her in her time of grief. However, towards the back of the group and obviously trying her very best to blend in with the wall, was Ruby. I walked over to her.

"Hi, Ruby, I'm really pleased that you were able to come today," I said.

Ruby smiled shyly and looked around awkwardly. "I have to be here," she said, her eyes downcast. The look on her face was one of abject misery.

Tomas started to usher the guests inside and I fell into step beside Ruby. I took a seat while Ruby went up to the coffin to say her goodbyes to Eric. She spoke quietly to him, leaned down and kissed his forehead and took a seat, tears streaming down her face. The other guests looked at her curiously but a part of me was pleased for her that she had the chance to say goodbye. I was also pleased that someone in this group was actually mourning for Eric. God knows I hadn't liked the man, but it just struck me as wrong that he lived almost thirty years on this Earth and nobody mourned his passing. Admittedly he wasn't the greatest human being that ever lived, but he was far from the worst. Maybe my family was right and I was just too soft hearted. According to my Grandma Rita that soft heart was going to get me into trouble one day.

The celebrant Tomas had organized for the funeral was very good. She had taken the small amount of information that I had given her about Eric, and managed to turn it into an uplifting and moving service. I kept checking on Adele and Ruby as they seemed to be the only two who were affected in any way. Adele sat there stony-faced, all signs of tears gone. In direct contrast, Ruby had gone from tears streaming down her face to deep heaving sobs. At the point where the celebrant asked if there was anyone who wanted to share their memories of Eric, I went to shake my head. To my surprise Ruby stood up and headed for the lectern. Adele looked at me inquiringly. I tried to nod encouragingly. Ruby stood at the front of the room and wiped her face with her arm.

"You don't know me but I grew up with Eric. He lived next door to me my entire life. He was always kind to me. He protected me when I needed it and he supported me. He was my best friend."

I could see Adele looking a little uncomfortable. Considering she had been married to him, she had only been able to say that she truly hated him. Then to have this young girl actually providing the kind of words she should have said, it was bound to make her feel uncomfortable.

"Eric was also my husband." My head snapped around and an audible gasp filled the room, which was quite an achievement considering how few people were in attendance. Tomas looked at me frantically for a sign as the celebrant made a step towards Ruby. Adele stood up and advanced towards the younger woman.

"What are you saying?" she said in a completely controlled voice, very unlike the emotional wreck I had been seeing the last few days.

"Eric and I got married six years ago when I was eighteen," Ruby said, a slight quiver in her voice but she lifted her head.

"That is not possible," Adele said. "It is not possible that I was in a bigamous marriage. He wouldn't dare do that to me."

Ruby looked at her. "He loved me. I was the only one he wanted to marry, but he needed money and said marrying you was the way he could get it."

By this point Tomas had given up looking for a way to fix this situation. Nobody wanted to make a move and interrupt the drama playing out in front of us.

"He was my husband and I loved him," declared Adele

and I looked on in shock. What happened to the woman who only twenty minutes ago was telling me how much she loathed the man in the coffin.

"I'm sorry," Ruby faltered and I cursed inwardly as I moved towards her.

I put my arm around her and moved her away from the podium and out the door. I could hear Tomas taking control of the situation inside while I led Ruby to the small memorial garden. As she sat in one of the garden seats and took in deep gulps of air while trying to hold back the sobs, I could see the abject misery on her face.

"Is it true?" I asked gently. "Were you really married to him?"

Ruby nodded and pulled a piece of paper out of her bag and handed it to me. I straightened the wrinkled piece of paper and saw that, indeed, six years ago Ruby Farrow and Eric Davis got married.

I sighed. "You don't by any chance have a divorce or annulment in there as well do you?" I asked, only half joking.

Ruby shook her head. I squatted down next to her. My heart went out to this poor girl. She had obviously adored Eric.

"I am so sorry that you lost him," I said gently. "Is there anyone I can call to come and get you?"

"No," she said and suddenly straightened up. "I can get home myself. I know he isn't there but I just wanted to say goodbye and to let those people know there was a good side to him. I know how they would have looked at him and I won't deny that Eric was selfish, but you know what, when my stepfather was on a rampage, Eric was the one who protected and hid me. When he got big and strong enough, he beat up my stepfather for daring to lay a hand on me. He did a lot of stupid things, but he could be a good man sometimes. I just wanted the people who thought he was dirt to know that."

Ruby turned and walked away and I just stood there.

She was right. We'd all just seen the one side of Eric that we wanted to see. Walking back into the funeral home I could see that the service had wrapped up fairly quickly after Ruby's revelation. I headed towards the reception area, but caught up in thinking about Ruby, I took a wrong turn and found myself looking out into a private courtyard. I pulled back suddenly when I saw that in the middle of the courtyard was Adele, locked in an embrace with Elliot Powell. He was holding her tightly and I saw him drop his head and place a tender kiss on her lips. I stepped back and hurriedly found the reception room. Unfortunately the first person I saw was Miranda Powell and as she headed towards me I just felt like I wanted to get away.

"There you are, Trudie," she said. "I wanted to thank you for dealing with that unfortunate situation during the funeral."

So Ruby was now an unfortunate situation. Good to know.

"I wish I could say I was surprised, but after the abominable way that man treated Adele, well nothing surprises me. I only hope that Adele can take the time to heal."

I was beginning to feel sick. Right at this moment Adele was kissing this woman's husband and she had no idea. I hate being in situations like this. I am one of those people that if my husband was cheating on me, I would want to know. That being said, being told by pretty much a complete stranger would really come at the top of my possible cringe worthy moments in life. In my head I kept repeating Monique's mantra for her personal assistants. The client's personal life is none of your business. As long as it does not put you in a legally compromising position don't judge and don't interfere. Right now, looking into this woman's face and knowing what her husband and best friend were doing, I was judging like you wouldn't believe, but I couldn't interfere.

I could, however, feel like throwing up when Elliot

Powell walked up to his wife and put an arm around her waist.

"Darling, I've been looking for you," he said as he dropped a kiss on the side of her cheek.

"Is Adele feeling better?" Miranda asked, a loving smile for her husband on her face.

"As good as can be expected," Elliot said sorrowfully.

"There she is now," I said, desperate to get away from the farce I was watching.

Chapter Twenty

As I walked towards Adele I noticed that Griffin and Ramos had entered the reception room as well. I smiled brightly at Griffin and was surprised by the answering frown.

"Adele Wesson," he said in a loud, commanding voice.

Everybody stopped and looked. Adele turned around.

"Adele Wesson," Griffin repeated. "You are under arrest for the murder of Eric Wesson."

While Griffin gave Adele her rights, Ramos grabbed her hands and handcuffed them behind her back. Elliot stepped forward with a visibly upset Miranda beside him.

"What is this all about?" he demanded.

"Exactly as I said, sir," Griffin said, standing between Adele and Elliot. "Mrs Wesson has been charged with the murder of her husband."

"I am her lawyer and I demand that you let me speak to my client."

"As soon as we process her down at the station, if she requests a lawyer, we will be contacting you. Until then, please do not interfere."

"Elliot," Adele said, the fear in her voice evident.

"I'll be there as soon as I can," said Elliot. "Do not say a word to anyone until I get there. Do you understand what I am saying?"

"Yes Elliot," Adele said as she was led away by Ramos.

Griffin swung around and followed her. "Miss Eyre, we are requesting that you attend the station to assist in our inquiries," he said, without even looking in my direction.

My jaw dropped as I watched him walk out the room. In an instant I had Tomas beside me.

"Don't do or say anything you are going to regret," he warned.

I looked at him, the anger at the way Griffin had spoken to me building up to the point where I was barely able to speak.

"Your face has gone some weird kind of color. I'm sure your friend didn't mean that the way it sounded."

Unfortunately, I think he did. Travis's words about Griffin came rushing back at me and all of a sudden I had a very bad feeling in the pit of my stomach. That feeling didn't leave me as I drove through the streets of LA. It was still there as I pushed through the doors of the station. It rose up into my throat when I was met by Ramos and led into yet another interrogation room. Looking around at the bare walls and the obligatory mirror I wondered how many more times I was going to end up in one of these rooms. Waiting alone in the room, I remembered that the last time I was stuck in here, Griffin had left me cooling my heels for almost an hour. A spurt of defiance went through me. If he thought I was going to wait for him again, he had another thing coming. I was rising out of the chair when Griffin walked into the room and sat down in the chair opposite me. I slowly lowered myself back into the seat and waited silently for him to start speaking.

"Trudie," he said.

"Really," I shot back. "At the funeral home I was Miss Eyre. Why the lack of formality now?"

Griffin grimaced. "Trudie, I'm in a difficult position. This is my case and as usual I'm finding you right in the middle of it."

"Not my fault," I said.

"No," he conceded. "But the fact of the matter is that I am trying to build a case and everywhere I turn, there you are. I have to tread very carefully."

"So, what is the problem? Why did you arrest Adele?"

"Last night we executed a search warrant on Adele Wesson's home. We found a gun in her safe."

"Why did you search last night? The place has been a crime scene for days."

"We didn't know about the safe until yesterday. It was missed in the original search."

"Then how did you find out about it...?" My voice trailed off. "You overheard me talking to Adele yesterday when you were at my home," I said. "You used that information for your search warrant."

"Yes, I did," Griffin said, looking me straight in the eye.

All of a sudden I realized something else. "The phone call last night. You weren't calling to talk to me, you were just making sure that I wasn't at Adele's house so you could do your search warrant without tipping her off."

Griffin nodded and that weird feeling in my stomach lurched up into my throat.

"Why were you really at the funeral home this morning?" I asked, part of me not wanting to hear and part of me needing to hear.

"We put surveillance equipment in the room as we wanted to capture anything that was said that could be incriminating. We weren't sure if we would be able to do it, normally access would be a problem," he said.

I continued for him. "But there I was and I told Tomas it was fine to have you there, not thinking for one moment that you could possibly be using me."

"I wasn't using you," said Griffin through gritted teeth.

I smiled coldly. "Yes, you were. Well, now you got precisely what you wanted, could you please explain to me why I am here?"

Griffin went to say something else, but took one look at my face and obviously thought better of it.

"We need to know if Adele knew about Eric's first wife."

"As far as I am aware she didn't know."

"Were you aware of Eric's first wife?"

"I only met Ruby for the first time yesterday. I informed her of the funeral believing her to be a friend. Her speech today was as much a surprise to me as it was to everyone else."

Griffin looked at me, expecting me to continue. Fat chance of that happening. I would answer his questions but that was it. No way was I trusting this man with any more information.

"On the morning of the murder we found gunshot residue on Adele's hands. Do you know of anywhere that she would have got the gunshot residue?"

"No."

"Do you believe Adele killed her husband?"

"No."

"Do you have any idea of anyone else who could have killed Eric Wesson?"

"No."

"Are you planning on answering any of my questions with anything other than a yes or no answer?"

"No."

"Dammit, Trudie. Stop being so stubborn. This is a murder case and it's a little more important than the fact you have got your feelings hurt. I did my job and I'd do it exactly the same again."

"Good to know," I said. "As you've got everything about today on tape I don't think there is any need for this to continue. I don't think Adele killed her husband but you know what, at the moment I'm having serious doubts about my intuition when it comes to the people I believe in. I have no idea who killed Eric. I do not have any further information that will help you, so talking to me is a complete waste of your time and my patience. If you have any further questions for me you can direct them to my lawyer, Reggie. I'm sure you remember him, because I know he remembers you."

With that I picked up my purse and headed for the door. Griffin jumped up and grabbed my arm.

"Trudie, don't be like this. You don't understand, I have a job to do."

I shook off his arm. "You're wrong," I said. "I

understand perfectly well. You used me. It may have been for all the right reasons but at the moment I don't like you very much. So, like I said, if you need to speak to me, do it through my lawyer."

Holding my head high I walked away, feeling his stare right between my shoulder blades but I'm proud to say I didn't falter, not at any point during the walk through the station, not on the car ride home and not on the walk into my apartment. I held it together as I peeled off my clothes and stepped into the shower. Only in there was I finally able to let go and for today it wasn't tears. No, I was angry, really angry. Part of me kept repeating that he was only doing his job but there was a bigger part of me that felt betrayed. I really wanted to hit something, preferably an arrogant detective, but wait a minute, I was never going to see that arrogant detective again. Once I had that thought the tears did start. After a good cathartic cry I found myself in my most comfortable sweats tucking into a large tub of ice cream.

An insistent knock on my door distracted me from the ice cream headache I was trying to give to myself. Looking at the door I just did not feel up to dealing with anyone and decided to ignore the knocking. It eventually stopped and I could hear footsteps walking away. I breathed a sigh of relief and got back to drowning my sorrows in the ice cream tub. Next thing I heard was those footsteps returning and the scratching of keys in the lock. I dropped my head, not even bothering to look up as Crystal walked in. She took one look at my position on the floor, in sweats that were so worn they could not be seen outside the front door and hugging a tub of ice cream, and shook her head as she grabbed a spoon and sat next to me.

"Those keys are only supposed to be used for emergencies," I said as she tried to grab a spoonful of ice cream.

"This obviously is an emergency," she said as she managed to fill her spoon. "So what did Detective Hottie do?"

"What makes you think it was him," I grumbled. "And anyway from now on he's Detective Dumbass."

"Ouch," Crystal grimaced. "What did he do?"

"He used me to make a case against my boss for murder."

"That's a new one," she said. "But what do you expect? All men are jerks only after one thing."

"Bad time?" Edwin said from the doorway.

"No, no," said Crystal, waving him in. "I was just saying men are jerks after one thing."

Edwin paused as he sat down. "You do realize that I am a man."

"Well yeah," said Crystal as she licked her spoon. "But I don't think of you as a man, not in the normal sense anyway."

I winced at Edwin's crestfallen look which he wiped away quickly. Crystal treated Edwin as her gay best friend. Unfortunately Edwin was very straight and had a crush on Crystal. He was also a struggling actor. Seeing as Crystal had struggling actors hitting on her all the time in the hope that she would cast them in a blockbuster movie, Edwin was biding his time until he made his own way in the acting world. Then he would pursue Crystal. The only stumbling block in this grand master plan that he had told me about one night, when he was very drunk, was that Edwin was a really bad actor. He was gorgeous, which was a point in his favor, but despite the endless acting lessons, the man gave new meaning to the word wooden. Unfortunately he hadn't quite worked that out for himself yet and I wasn't ready to destroy his dreams, so the three of us went ahead as if everything was perfectly normal.

"So what man is proof that the entire gender is worthless," Edwin said as he grabbed his own spoon.

"Detective Dumbass," Crystal said, still licking the spoon with Edwin watching her avidly.

"I thought we were going with Detective Hottie."

"Not anymore, not after what he's done," Crystal said with relish as Edwin passed the tub of ice cream to her with a look of anticipation on his face.

I grabbed it and wrenched it back.

Edwin frowned. "So what did Detective Dumbass do that was so terrible that he is being held up as an example of all that is wrong with men?"

I looked at him sourly. "You know you weren't invited."

"Yes, well, I'm pretty sure that Crystal wasn't invited either, but here we are. Just look at us as your own personal therapy session, full of judgment and bad advice."

"He overheard something Adele said to me on the phone and used it to get some incriminating evidence from her house. He called me last night to make sure that I wasn't near Adele's house so he could do a search warrant, and he bugged Eric's coffin today by using me to get access to the funeral home. He did all this without telling me."

Edwin looked at me quizzically. "Hasn't he just done his job? He's a cop looking for a murderer, isn't he supposed to do anything it takes."

Both Crystal and I looked at him.

"Or not. Bad Detective Dumbass." He popped a spoon of ice cream in his mouth.

"Look," I said, "logically I know he was just doing his job, but right at this moment I feel used. I thought something special was happening between us but now I feel like he betrayed me."

"I understand," said Crystal.

Edwin popped up an eyebrow.

"No, hear me out. I had a date last night with a guy and we started talking about what constituted cheating in a relationship. He was telling me that as a guy he doesn't think kissing is even close to cheating. And I said that it didn't matter what he thought constituted cheating. If I'm the girlfriend, it matters what I think is cheating, because it is about my feelings and how hurt and betrayed I felt. That's exactly the same here. Detective Dumbass thinks what he did was the right thing, but you feel hurt and betrayed. Doesn't matter what he thinks because it's your feelings at play here. It only matters what you feel. If you can't deal with what he's done, then it is better that you give him the flick."

She sat back, proud of her analogy and looked expectantly at Edwin and me.

"What?" she said, looking confused at our expressions.

"No," I said, "your thinking is sound. I'm just wondering why you are discussing what constitutes cheating on a first date. Were you guys establishing some ground rules for the future or something?"

"No, of course not. I worked out I wasn't seeing him again within the first thirty seconds."

"Then why didn't you leave?" I ventured.

"Are you kidding, they make the best dates when there is no trying to impress while you are holding out for a future date. I get to have the most awesome conversations. I start asking questions and next thing I know guys just start letting it all hang out."

"And you think that is a good thing," I said slowly.

"It's great," Crystal said. "When both of you know that it's not going anywhere but you're still willing to finish the date it means you can say anything."

"Which brings us to a conversation on cheating on the first date."

"Exactly, so you have no cause to feel you are being unreasonable. It's about how you are feeling. That's all that is important."

"You have anything to add to Dr Phil over there," I said to Edwin.

"No, I think she got it all. Anyway you've got us and you've got ice cream. What more could you possibly need."

Chapter Twenty-One

I kept repeating Edwin's advice as I sat in the courtroom the next day across from Griffin at Adele's bail arraignment. I had debated whether to attend the hearing, but I had been with Adele every step of the way, and just because I wanted to spend the day huddled under my blankets, didn't mean I was going to desert her now. I had to deal with the situation at hand. Unfortunately my situation at hand was a client who was charged with the murder of her husband.

Elliot and Miranda Powell came through the courthouse doors and I smiled tentatively at them. Miranda smiled back and Elliot nodded his head at me. They sat closer to the front of the courtroom, probably trying to make sure that Adele knew they were there. Surprisingly Travis also turned up and slid into the seat beside me. I could see Griffin frowning when he saw the two of us but I ignored him.

"What are you doing here?" I hissed.

"I was a witness in a case earlier. Saw this was on the docket so thought I'd have a look."

"You know, considering you are not being paid for this you seem to be spending an awful lot of time following this case," I said.

"Just curious I guess. Gotta say, did not see this coming at all. I assumed I'd get another phone call, find Eric with his pants down and a quick and expensive divorce. Would never have guessed that she had it in her to off her husband."

"She might not have been the one to kill him," I whispered back.

"I don't know," said Travis. "Much as I don't like the guy, Griffin is pretty good at his job. I don't think he would have charged her unless he had some compelling evidence."

I stared ahead stonily. Travis looked at me speculatively. "And he used you to get the evidence didn't he?"

I glared at him.

"Told you he was all about the job. You need to not be in the way when he is after someone or he will roll right over the top of you."

"You're going with an 'I told you so' now," I said, letting my annoyance show.

"Oh, honey, believe me, I wish for your sake it could have been different but at least you found out what he is like now rather than later."

"Well thank you," I said sarcastically. "Now maybe I should start working for you and lose all my faith in humanity."

"Wouldn't want that," Travis murmured, and as I looked in his eyes I saw seriousness for a change.

At that moment Adele was led into the courtroom. She looked frail. Jail was not going to work for her. Without her makeup and wardrobe she looked fragile and delicate.

Travis let out a breath. "She's not looking good is she?"

I shook my head. If this was how much she deteriorated after only one night, I didn't see her being able to hold up for much longer. Watching the legal arguments being made between the prosecutor and the hotshot criminal lawyer that Elliot had organized, I suddenly felt tired. The legal arguments were over quickly and bail was set. Elliot and Miranda hustled Adele out of the courtroom and whisked her away, probably to a drug induced sleep.

"Want a coffee?" Travis nudged me as I stood up.

"Sure," I said and followed him out.

Sitting in the diner, Travis leaned back and studied me.

"What?" I said. "Do I have something on my face?"

"You don't believe she did it do you?"

"No," I said.

"Why not?"

"Probably because I'm a trusting idiot," I said tiredly.

"Even trusting idiots need a reason," said Travis. "What is yours?"

"Adele is deathly afraid of spiders, hates them with a passion."

"Okay, but what does that have to do with anything?" Travis asked.

"One morning when I came into work, Adele was hunched in a corner. There was a spider on her desk and she was absolutely freaking out. I was going to kill it for her when she stopped me, asked me to catch it, drive twenty miles and release it."

"Seems a bit extreme," Travis said.

"The point I'm trying to make is that she hated that spider, wanted it gone but even then she would not let me kill it. At the moment I'm the last person to say that the woman is a saint, but I really don't think she has it in her to stand next to Eric, shoot a bullet into his head and then crawl into bed beside him and go to sleep."

"Does sound a bit unlikely," conceded Travis as he took a sip of coffee. "Griffin must have some serious evidence if he believes that Adele is the killer."

"As far as I know they found the gun in Adele's safe, gun residue on her hands and they've got a recording of a discussion Adele and I had next to Eric's coffin, where she told me that she hated him and that it was a good thing he was dead."

Travis raised an eyebrow.

"I know, out of context it sounds bad. I mean it didn't sound good in context either, but I still don't think she did it."

"Where would you go next if you were looking into it?"

"I'd probably speak to Eric's other wife."

Travis choked on his coffee.

"Another wife?" he queried as he grabbed a napkin and

started to wipe up his shirt.

"Yes, it seems that Eric married Ruby, the neighbor we saw the other day, about six years ago. Didn't divorce her, so legally he was still married to her. She turned up at the funeral yesterday and gave a little speech."

"Must have been interesting."

"Yes it was. I had a short chat with her yesterday but this was all before Adele got arrested. I didn't ask her too many questions. She was hurting. Seems she really loved the jerk."

I slumped back in my seat.

"Not feeling quite so idealistic at the moment?" Travis queried.

"I'm just dandy," I replied with a forced smile.

"Don't do that," Travis said, leaning over the table.

"Do what?" I queried.

"That fake smile thing. Tell me what's going on."

"What are you, a shrink?"

Travis smiled widely. "Honey, I've had so many women and men crying on my shoulder, I should be board certified by now."

"You're seriously disturbed, you know that," I said, a smile teasing itself out.

"And there's the smile that I wanted," said Travis as he stood up. "Okay, so if we want to find out what really happened to Eric, the next stop is the other wife. You want to come with me?"

"Why are you looking into this?" I asked as I got up. "Surely you have better things to do than look into a closed murder case."

"Usually I do, but as of this morning I have been hired by Elliot Powell to find any and all information which will provide the defense with reasonable doubt against the charges facing Adele Wesson."

"For the love of… You were pumping me for information," I said, getting annoyed. "Seriously, can I not find one man who is actually interested in my company and not what I may or may not know about a murder?"

Travis grabbed my arm and turned me around. "Firstly I am very interested in your company, with or without the drama that seems to surround you. Secondly, I hadn't officially taken the case yet. I wanted to get your opinion on the situation before I said yes." He pulled out his phone. "Now if you don't want me to take the case I will text Maria and tell her we're not interested. If you want to help me with the case I will text Maria to send the paperwork through and officially take it on. My next step is your choice, honey."

I looked up at him, confused. "Why is it my choice? What I want should have nothing to do with your business decisions."

"It doesn't have anything to do with my business decisions. However, I like hearing your opinion. You sometimes see things in a way that I may have become too cynical to see. It's kind of refreshing and sometimes I like seeing the world in the same way that you do. Anyway, at least this is a bit of a change from taking photos of men with their pants around their ankles."

I laughed suddenly. "You are a very strange man," I said. "Take the case. I think Adele needs as much help as she can get."

Travis shot off a quick text. "Very well then, we need to get to the other wife's house."

"What do you mean, we? Surely you don't want me interfering."

"You would be wrong," Travis said. "You've already established a relationship with her. She is more likely to talk if you are there with me. Also I sometimes have a problem in that women find me intimidating."

"Really," I said sarcastically. "I can't imagine why that would be."

"Ha ha," said Travis as he stopped next to a car and opened the passenger door.

I took one look at the car and burst out laughing.

Travis's current ride was a little compact that was about twenty years old and bright canary yellow.

"Just get in," he said, slamming the door behind me as I got in the seat, still laughing and wiping my eyes.

The car's interior was a horrendous brown color and the look on his face as he squeezed himself into the small car was priceless and sent me into peals of laughter again. Starting the engine up, his knee banging against the steering wheel, he sat stony faced.

"I thought the cars you drove were supposed to blend in," I said, still smiling.

"That's true but my car got totaled a couple of days ago thanks to this case and this was the only other car that I had available" replied Travis.

"Why do you have it? It looks like a rubber ducky on wheels. Not exactly the blending in type of vehicle."

"Every now and then we want someone to know that they are being followed or I need a decoy car," said Travis. "Rubber ducky on wheels works for those times."

"I'm amazed you actually fit in it," I said.

"I don't really, we had to bust the springs in the driver's seat to give me a bit of head room."

I burst out laughing again. Looking up, as I wiped the tears out of my eyes, I saw Travis smiling at me as he smoothly pulled into the street.

Chapter Twenty-Two

Sitting on Ruby's couch, my heart went out to the poor girl. The second she started talking to us about Eric she had dissolved into tears. Travis's face had taken on that panicked look that most men get when faced with a woman crying. Looking at him in disgust I got up and sat next to the poor girl, putting my arm around her shoulders and had her sobbing into my chest.

"I'm so sorry," I said repeatedly, and I was.

I never liked Eric but there must have been something in him that made him special to Ruby. Wiping her eyes she sniffed.

"I know what people think of Eric," she said quietly. "We grew up without any money at all. He never wanted to go back to that. He wanted to have money, it was all he worried about. He knew women found him attractive and they would always throw gifts at him, things he could never afford otherwise. He figured if he just kept taking the money until he could get a good amount together, then he could buy a gym himself and then he wouldn't need to answer to anyone. We could get started with our life together then."

Travis cleared his throat. "Why would he marry Adele Wesson if he was already married to you?"

I choked on the temptation to tell the insensitive male in the room to shut up, but Ruby proved stronger than I thought she would.

"He thought being married to one of these rich women would be his big score. He just needed to find one dumb enough not to get a prenup."

I winced. That did sound pretty accurate.

"That didn't bother you at all?" pushed Travis.

"Knowing he was going to be with another woman, that he was married to another woman."

"Of course it bothered me," Ruby said, once again on the verge of tears. "But Eric told me that what he did physically with those women meant nothing. He was doing it for our future. I would always be the only one who really knew him, the only one that he really loved. Everything else was just a way of getting money. He was doing it all for us."

She dissolved into tears again.

"Please," she said. "I know you're working for her. If she did this to Eric, please don't help her go free. I know what people think of him but if she killed him, it wasn't right. She shouldn't get away with it just because she's rich."

"Is there anyone else that you know of that could have done it, someone who Eric may have hurt?" Travis asked.

Ruby smiled through her tears.

"Women don't like being used for their money, even when they know what the score is. Eric always had women mad at him, and if it wasn't the women it was their husbands or boyfriends."

"Do you have any names or anything that we can follow up on?" Travis asked.

"No," said Ruby. "Eric never wanted any of that part of his life to touch me. He didn't want me to know what he was doing, he didn't want me to be hurt by it."

"Was there anyone else that he would have confided in?"

Ruby thought carefully for a moment. "His friend, Anton. Anton and he have been friends since they were kids. Anton got him the job at that high class gym that Eric worked at before he met Adele. If anyone knows about the women Eric was with, it would be Anton."

Leaving Ruby I didn't look at Travis as I got in the car.

"You know, I don't know whether those two had a devoted relationship or whether she was a completely delusional fool," Travis said heavily. "You knew Eric for a little while. Could you see that side of him?"

"No," I said. "As far as I was concerned he was a gold digger with the morals of an alley cat. Dealing with him was the worst part of my day at work."

Travis nodded "Ruby seems to be sweet. If he was taking advantage of her it kind of takes him to a whole new level of lowlife."

I nodded in agreement.

"Ready to tackle Anton?" Travis asked cheerfully.

I smiled and before I could answer my phone rang. Looking at the caller ID I could see that it was Griffin. My smile faded. Without thinking about it I hit the reject button and put the phone back in my bag.

"Griffin?" queried Travis.

I looked at him startled. "How did you know?"

"Trained investigator remember," he smiled.

"Yes."

"So you're at the ignoring his phone calls stage of the relationship."

"I don't even know if what we had could be called a relationship," I said glumly.

"You're mad," Travis observed.

"Yes I am and don't you start telling me I'm being unreasonable."

"Hey, sister, I already told you I think the guy is a douchebag."

I smiled. "Bit harsh, don't you think? I thought guys stuck up for each other when it came to women."

"Not all the time. Sometimes even men can see when a guy's being a jerk. Or sometimes they want the girl themselves and are just looking for the opportunity to take his place."

"Really?" I questioned.

"Do you have any idea the number of people who find out their significant other is also doing their best friend?" Travis said, a grin on his face.

"You are just a whole new level of depressing aren't you?" I said.

"I'm serious, it happens all the time, and I'm not even going to start on how many times it's the sister or brother."

"Stop talking please? Every time you start I get a little more demoralized about the way that the world is."

"So you should," nodded Travis sagely, a small smile playing on his lips.

The gym that Anton worked in was completely removed from the one that we had been to for Eric previously. The place screamed money and sophistication. The people who were working out were wearing designer gym clothes and even some high price jewelry. I could see how Eric would think he'd hit the jackpot by working here. Getting to the reception area I was surprised to find Edwin behind the desk.

"What are you doing here?" I asked before Travis could start speaking.

"Temp job," said Edwin. I shouldn't have been surprised. Looking around the place at the mostly female clientele and the incredibly muscular and gorgeous, predominantly male, staff, I could see how Edwin had landed the job.

"What are you doing here, Trudie? Thinking of signing up?" Edwin asked.

I allowed myself a quick fantasy of swanning around the gym, attaining that perfect body surrounded by gorgeous male personal trainers. Alas, a moment was all I could give that particular fantasy, before reality and my love for chocolate intruded.

"Not today," I said, watching as one particularly muscular specimen of manhood walked past me in the tiniest of shorts.

Behind me I could here Travis snorting but to his credit Edwin, despite knowing that my willpower when it came to fitness was never the best, kept a completely straight face.

"We were wondering if we could speak to Anton."

"Any reason in particular?" Edwin asked curiously.

"He was a friend of Eric Wesson. We are just doing some follow up for Adele."

"Don't see a problem with that," said Edwin as he pressed down on an intercom system and called for Anton.

"Here he comes," said Edwin.

I turned around and felt like I was stunned. Anton was masculine perfection. His body was not overly big, but it showed the hours that he spent in the gym in all their glory.

"Close your mouth, you're drooling," whispered Travis.

I felt my hand reaching for my face when I realized who said it. My eyes narrowed.

"I hate you."

"Not the first time you've said it," Travis grinned.

"Maybe not," I stated. "But I think it needs repeating."

"What's up?" Anton directed at Edwin.

"These people need to speak to you," said Edwin, waving a hand in our direction and then turning his attention to the computer again.

"What can I do for you?" asked Anton.

"Is there somewhere private we can talk?" asked Travis.

"This way," said Anton and led us into one of the locker rooms. There was a distinct citrus scent in the air which masked the stale sweat odor that I usually associated with gyms.

"So what's this about?" Anton asked.

Travis pulled out a card. "My name's Travis Cooper and this is Trudie Eyre."

I smiled warmly, maybe a bit too warmly from the look Travis gave me.

"We are looking into the death of Eric Wesson and we were told that you were good friends with Eric."

Anton sat down heavily on a chair.

"Yeah, Eric was my best friend from when we were kids. Always got into trouble with each other. Always got ourselves out of it too. Can't believe some woman killed him, especially not that rich woman he married. No way did she seem the type."

"We heard that you got Eric a job here before he met Adele," Travis said.

"Yeah, Eric was the type they like working here. This place isn't too bad but it caters for a certain type of clientele. Management like us to keep the customer very happy, if you know what I mean."

Travis and I nodded. Travis because he understood, me because I didn't want to understand.

"Eric met Adele here, she wasn't really into the exercise side of things but then not many of them are. She fell for him pretty hard and he married her."

"Even though he was already married to Ruby?" I interrupted.

"Oh, you know about Ruby," Anton said.

"Yes we do, Ruby came to the funeral. Made for quite a scene," I said. "First funeral I've been to where both of the wives turned up."

"Look, you got to understand where we came from. We had no money, none at all. And then you have these women who have got so much money and they're willing to spend it on us. We're not going to turn it down, not when all they want is some attention. That's the way it started with Eric and Adele. She was buying him all this stuff but she wanted more and more attention. She needed it. The more Eric gave her, the more she wanted and then she wanted him to make it into a relationship. All Eric could see was that this could be the big payday for him. If he could pull this off, give up a year or two of his life and he could take care of himself and Ruby for years."

"So, he hadn't ditched Ruby?" asked Travis.

"No," said Anton. "If there was anyone that Eric loved, it was Ruby."

He obviously saw the disbelief on my face.

"Look, Eric was no saint. He liked women, sex and money and not necessarily in that order but, and this is something you have to remember, he loved Ruby as much as someone that damaged could love anyone. His mother did a number on him and his priorities were completely screwed up. He was a good friend to me and I will miss him. He treated most women like crap, but he treated Ruby like a princess. Most of his drive to get more money was so he could set up a life with Ruby."

"But he was sleeping with so many women," I said. "How could he reconcile that with being in love with Ruby?"

"To him sex meant nothing, it was a tool to get what he wanted and he wanted money fast. Adele was nothing more to Eric than a cash machine. He once told me that the more he fooled around on Adele, the more money and gifts she threw at him."

Well that explained Eric's constant sleeping around.

"Any of the women get upset at the lack of feeling on Eric's part?" Travis asked.

"Most of the women here know the score and usually they have husbands at home who are providing them with the money they need to give to Eric. They don't want anything that is going to actually interfere with their nice little setup."

"Husbands then."

"Could be. He never told me about any husbands that he had problems with, but that doesn't mean there weren't any," Anton said.

"Any way we could find out?" Travis asked.

Anton went to a locker in the corner and opened it, pulling out a keychain which had a tag attached to it. He passed it to Travis. "Look, this is a key to a place that Eric kept. The address is on the tag. He never wanted anything he did to taint Ruby, so he kept this place as a home that was separate to her. If there was anything going on in

Eric's life that was going to get him killed, chances are that it would be there."

"Thanks," said Travis, grasping the key.

"Eric wasn't a bad guy," insisted Anton. "He just never had a chance."

Chapter Twenty-Three

I considered what Anton had said as we drove to the apartment that matched the key.

"So what are you thinking?" Travis asked.

"Just about Anton and Ruby. Before this I would not have thought for an instant that there was anyone who would say a nice thing about Eric. As far as I was concerned he was just a horny jerk out to drain as much money as he could from Adele."

"Not everyone is good or bad, most people have shades of gray in them," Travis said. "Good people do some pretty rotten things sometimes, and people we see as bad usually have someone who believes they hung the moon. When I was working as a cop the number of bad guys we had whose mother's swore they were really good kids. It would be easier to believe that people are either good or bad. They're not, they're just people. Unfortunately Eric spent his life playing games with other people's feelings. That kind of thing is a surefire way to get yourself into a world of hurt. Most murders, regardless of who it is, come down to sex, drugs, money or crazy, or a combination of those four. So far Eric was playing fast and loose with sex and money. That makes him a prime candidate for a violent end. What we have to do is find out whether they actually did contribute to his death."

I nodded, still finding it hard to reconcile the Eric that I had heard about with the Eric that I knew. Standing in his apartment putting on the gloves that Travis insisted I should wear, I was forced to reevaluate again. I had expected a flashy bachelor pad. Instead the apartment was subdued in earth colored tones, nothing like how I would have pictured Eric's love nest. The bed in the center of the apartment was huge and I looked away from it, feeling I was invading Eric's privacy, when Travis jumped on top of it and reached up to the light fitting above the bed.

"What are you doing?" I asked, a little concerned at his behavior.

Travis looked over his shoulder at me as he started to unscrew the mirrored light fitting. "Just a hunch," he said. Putting the fitting on the bed next to him he reached up again. "Just like I thought," he said and passed me a tiny little black box.

Turning it over, I had an awful feeling in my stomach.

"It's a camera isn't it?" I said.

"Looks like it, which means that somewhere around here we should be able to find some home movies."

I dropped my head. "I should have remembered. I was beginning to think he might have been an okay guy."

"Best case scenario, the videos were consensual and were just a turn on for him and the women he was with."

"Worst case scenario?" I asked.

"Worst case scenario was Eric was screwing women with money and something to lose. He was then blackmailing them to generate another income stream."

"If the women knew about the camera why would it be hidden in the light fixture?" I asked.

"That's why I think we are closer to worst case scenario than best case scenario," Travis said.

"So where would these videos be?" I asked.

"Hopefully somewhere here," said Travis as he walked towards the desk in the corner of the apartment where a laptop was sitting. "Everything is computer based these days. If he was making videos and considering what we know about Eric I'm going to go out on a limb and assume that he was making a lot of videos, he would need a pretty big hard drive to hold it all."

I closed my eyes. "You don't think he uploaded it to the cloud?" I asked.

"No," Travis said thoughtfully as he started tapping the

keyboard of the laptop. "I think that Eric was too smart and had too focused a plan to allow control over these videos to go elsewhere. I would think that he would have set something up himself. There's a password on the computer, I can't get in."

"Can't you hack it or something?" I asked.

"No, sweetheart. Despite the many skills you seem to think that I possess, hacking is not one of them."

"You might want to look at that," I said. "Never too late to learn a new skill. Who knows? One day you may want to move on from catching men with their pants around their ankles."

"Not always men, sweetheart."

"I'm sure it isn't," I murmured, pretty sure that if we found the information recorded by those cameras it was going to be mostly women we found.

Looking at the big screen television, I noticed the network cord going into the wall. Looking around I spotted the walk in closet. Grabbing a chair I went over to the closet, opened the door and climbed on the chair.

"What are you doing?" asked Travis as he came over.

"Just got a hunch," I said as I reached toward the back of the top shelf of the closet. Standing on tiptoe I started pulling cords out of the hard drive and pulled it down.

"One hard drive," I said.

"How did you know?" asked Travis.

"The guy has a computer and a pretty sweet looking entertainment center. The television is hooked up somewhere and so is the computer, but I can't see any other equipment. Means he has got a network system somewhere. The only place really out of sight but also with enough air circulating for the equipment is his wardrobe. The back of the top shelf is out of sight but you can see conduit coming from the ceiling. If he was going to watch these movies on the big screen, and frankly all I know about Eric says that he's the kind to do that, he needs the drive to be connected to a network and here it is."

"Smart," said Travis.

"Or just lucky," I said. "One of my clients had a setup similar to this. All the televisions and computers were networked to a single hard drive, that way he could watch the movies on them from any screen in his house."

"Probably got a password on it," said Travis.

"It could," I said. "But I know an IT guy who says that people may, if you're lucky, put a password on the network, but they rarely put one on a removable hard drive like this. They get complacent thinking the security on the network will protect them. What they don't realize is that you can take the hard drive and connect it to another computer and there is no security at all."

"Let's have a look," said Travis, grabbing his backpack and pulling out a laptop.

Sitting at the table in the apartment he hooked up the hard drive and within seconds was looking at the file structure.

"Looks like we got lucky," he said and opened up a file.

Within seconds the moans of a woman started echoing through the room. Sure enough, there was Eric with a woman that was not either of his wives.

"Do you want to turn it off?" I said, keeping my eyes above the screen.

Travis grinned. "Not interested?"

"No, we know what it's about, don't need to see anymore. Chances are that woman had no idea she was being taped. It's wrong to watch it."

"You know, I didn't think women were that uptight anymore."

"I'm sure the women that you date aren't," I said.

Travis turned off the movie. Looking at the file structure I could see dozens of films on the hard drive.

"So what do we do with this?" I asked.

"We give it to the police," said Travis.

"Aren't you going to use it to solve the case?" I was a bit confused.

"Not my job, sweetheart. My job was simply to create reasonable doubt. I'll follow it and make sure that the police are actually pursuing other lines of inquiry, but other than that, I have done what I need to do. It's up to Griffin now, with me looking over his shoulder of course."

"Great, that's going to make him happy."

"I know, but I've got to say that I look at making Griffin's life difficult as one of the perks of the job."

While Travis made the phone call to Griffin I scrolled through the number of files on the hard drive. Travis finished up his phone call.

"Griffin will be here soon. We need to stay to answer questions. The guy is seriously annoyed that we found this place." All of this was said with a massive grin on his face.

When I didn't smile back Travis's grin dimmed. "What's the problem?"

"Look I knew that Eric had the morals of an alley cat, I knew the guy was gorgeous and charming, I just…all these women trusted him and look what happened."

"Sometimes you trust the wrong person," Travis said. "It happens all the time. When that trust is betrayed you can't let that damage who you are or the jerk wins."

I nodded. "So exactly how angry is Griffin?"

"I could almost see the steam coming through the phone. Got to say, that made my day. Almost willing to do the job for free for the chance to one up Griffin on his case." Travis's smile was back.

"You are an extremely petty man," I said smiling. "How much of a difference will this make to Adele's case, really?"

"Even with the gun the case against Adele was always going to be pretty circumstantial. By finding this hard drive the pool of suspects has now become huge. Every one of those women has a motive to kill Eric, not to mention husbands, boyfriends, and fathers. We have just thrown a major lot of reasonable doubt on the table. I don't see them going after Adele until they can clear that from the defense lawyers arsenal, and that is going to take a long time."

Chapter Twenty-Four

The knock at the door surprised me.

"That was quick," I said as Travis got the door.

Before he opened it he turned to me. "Just a word of warning, Griffin is really angry, he might put us in handcuffs."

"Not the first time," I muttered.

Travis raised an eyebrow and realizing what I had said, I went bright red. Travis opened the door and Jake Griffin walked in to find Travis laughing uproariously and my face looking like a tomato.

"Having fun," he drawled, looking at me piercingly.

"Best time I've had in ages," said Travis, giving me a big wink.

Griffin stiffened perceptively. I rolled my eyes at Travis, knowing that he had made the comment just to annoy Griffin.

"So what exactly is it that you think is so important to my case that I am racing down here?" Griffin stiffened his shoulders and directed his question towards Travis. I felt a little annoyed as he turned away from me.

"This is Eric Wesson's apartment which was used for some of his extramarital activities," Travis said, leaning back against the wall.

"Interesting," said Griffin. "And why exactly am I finding the two of you here?"

I decided that I really wasn't happy with being faced with Griffin's back.

"We spoke to a friend of Eric who told us about this place and gave us a key," I said.

Finally, Griffin turned towards me and going by the look on his face I was beginning to think that I should have kept my mouth shut.

"So you both thought that breaking and entering was a good idea."

"We were given a key by someone who had free access to the place," Travis interrupted.

"Kind of shaky ground there," Griffin said.

I held my breath waiting to see where this went next.

"So what did you have to tell me?" asked Griffin. "I'm assuming, considering it looks like the two of you are working together, that you have something that is supposed to blow my case against Adele out of the water."

"Just trying to help local law enforcement," said Travis.

"Of course you are," said Griffin, putting his full attention back on Travis. "And exactly why did you feel the need to pull Trudie into your investigation? It wouldn't have anything to do with your desperate need to annoy me would it?"

"Hey," I said, sure that somewhere in there I had been insulted. "I'm helping him. Adele is my employer. I do have something to contribute to this case. You were the first one to recognize that. If I wasn't so useful you wouldn't have used me to make your case."

Griffin looked as though he was about to answer my arguments when Travis interrupted.

"Much as I would enjoy this reality show playing itself out, I think Griffin might be a bit more interested in what we found."

I shrugged. Considering how Griffin seemed to prioritize everything below his work, Travis was probably correct. Moving over to the computer, Travis opened up one of the files and the next thing we heard was a woman's voice giving Eric some very explicit instructions. Much as I tried to be cool about it and portray an air of sophistication, I could feel the heat rising up my neck and knew that I was fighting a losing battle. Glancing up I saw Griffin looking at me speculatively and I could feel the blush deepen. Thankfully Travis turned off the file and the voices stopped.

Travis cleared his throat. "The hard drive we found has lots of files on them like that. I'm sure if you looked hard enough, you'd be able to find quite a few people who wanted Eric dead."

"It doesn't matter," said Griffin, still looking intently at me. "We found the gun in Adele's safe, she had gun residue on her hands and she was with the victim when he died. Her motive is still the strongest available."

"Still got reasonable doubt here and you know it. Do you really want to mess up your golden boy status by screwing up a high profile case like this?" Travis asked.

That statement got Griffin's attention. "You think I only care about a win, regardless of who did the actual killing?"

"I think that you have a tendency to get so focused on one person that you fail to see what else is going on around you," Travis said, smiling tightly.

Watching the two of them, I wondered how they had ever worked together.

At that moment Ramos walked in, took in the scene in front of her and with a muttered "oh hell" stepped between the two males who looked for all the world as if they were going to lock horns.

Catching the eye of her partner she asked quietly, "Do we have a problem here?"

Griffin sighed. "We could have. We need to seize all the electronic equipment here and do a search."

"I'll organize the paperwork," she said in her same quiet voice.

Travis tapped her on the shoulder and Ramos stiffened.

"You might want to include this," he said, holding up the small camera.

"Do I want to know where you found that?" Ramos asked.

"Light fitting above the bed," he said proudly.

"You're a pain in my neck, you know that don't you?" said Ramos.

"Of course I do, darling."

Ramos smiled tightly. "Call me darling again and I'll shoot you. Considering the way certain cops feel about you, I'd get away with it too."

Smiling again Travis walked towards the door.

"Coming, sweetheart?" he said, throwing a glance in my direction.

Muttering beneath my breath I followed him through the door, aware that Griffin was watching my every move. Once out of sight of the two cops I punched Travis in the arm.

"What was that?" I asked, my annoyance clear in my voice.

Travis doubled over laughing. "Did you see him?" he asked. "There was almost steam coming out of his ears. Oh, that moment was pure gold. Do you want a job because I think that would be the icing on the cake that would give Griffin a brain explosion?"

I shook my head. "You're not being nice," I said. "There isn't a need to cause that kind of a problem."

"The guy is uptight, always has been, always will be. The thing is that you shake him up. That little scene in there, that was because of you, not me. Griffin and I have butted heads too many times before to count. He has never taken it this personally. You are the difference here."

"I can't help that," I said, suddenly realizing that this conversation was taking an uncomfortable turn.

"I've seen Griffin with women before," Travis said as he leaned against his car. "None of them got under his skin the way you seem to. I'm not sure why but you seem to have found a chink in his perfect armor. You are the one who puts the golden boy off his game and I find that very interesting."

I mirrored his stance and crossed my arms. "You know, I think you just insulted me and I'm not sure why."

"Honey," Travis said as he opened my door for me. "Believe me when I say that was not an insult. In fact, I am in awe of whatever power you seem to possess."

"Great," I said.

After we'd been driving for a while I had to know. "Why do you dislike Griffin so much?"

Travis gave me a sideways glance and smiled.

"You know we were partners."

I nodded.

"One night we were chasing a suspect and we got separated. The suspect came at me suddenly and I wasn't able to get at my gun. He was hyped up on drugs and I was barely able to fight him off. He went down, hit his head on the pavement and died. Unfortunately he was some rich kid whose parents came after me. There was an investigation. Griffin refused to back my version of events. According to what I heard he believed that it was possible to talk this kid down and he felt I could have handled it differently. I got cleared but thanks to Griffin, there was always going to be a dark cloud over me. I wasn't asking him to lie, just to back me up. He wouldn't even do that. I quit the force the day I was cleared."

"Are you using me to get back at him? I understand if you're angry with him, but I'm not going to get into the middle of your little war. I'm really not that interested. In fact I'd be happy not to see either one of you ever again if that's the case."

With that I got out of the car and shut the door. As I opened the door to my apartment I heard him drive off. Closing the door I breathed a sigh of relief. My phone started ringing and looking down I saw it was Griffin again. Sighing, I answered the phone.

"What?" I said.

There was a pause. "Look, I know you're angry with me but working with Travis is a very bad idea."

I sighed. "I'm not angry anymore," I said. "I'm just really not interested in getting in the middle of this thing that the two of you have going on."

I could almost hear him grinding his teeth.

"Look, I'll come over and we can talk about this."

"No," I said quickly, "I've got to go out and get some work done."

"Trudie," he said, but it was too late. I hung up the phone.

Some women might enjoy being fought over by two men. Me, I knew what happened when male pride got involved. The situation became less about the woman and more about winning. I was not built like a trophy girlfriend and I was really not interested in becoming someone that was won. Grabbing my car keys I immediately headed out. I figured Griffin would not carry out his threat to come and see me, but just in case he did, I didn't want to be there. Admittedly once I'd gone through a drive-through and sat in a parking lot eating a burger, the thought that I may be acting a little cowardly went through my mind.

Jake Griffin confused me. I had never felt this on edge with anyone before in my life. When he looked at me and his eyes crinkled I just felt like melting where I stood, and when he took me in his arms I felt safe and on fire all at once. The problem was I had seen women who had fallen for men like him before. Men who put their work first over everything. In my family it was often joked that the women would only put up with men who adored them. I wanted to be adored, I wanted to be put first and if I couldn't have that then I didn't want anyone. As I was wiping the grease from my hands my phone rang again. Sighing I grabbed it without looking at the caller ID.

"Trudie," Adele's wavering voice came through. I was instantly on alert.

"Adele, what's going on?" I asked.

"Trudie, I need you to come to my house. I found something and I don't know what to do."

"What is it Adele?"

"I think I know why Eric was killed. I don't know who to turn to. You're the only one I trust."

Chapter Twenty-Five

Racing up the steps to Adele's house I called out her name.

"In here," she cried out.

I found her in the kitchen with her laptop open. The look on her face was devastated.

"How am I going to tell him?" she said, tears rolling down her face.

Making my way around to her side, I looked down at the computer screen. I recognized the bed in the paused video, I recognized the room and unfortunately I recognized both of the participants. There, frozen on the screen, was Eric Wesson and Miranda Powell.

"Oh no," I breathed.

"Elliot will be devastated if he sees this," Adele said.

I didn't feel that this was the appropriate time to remind her of the rather close clinch I had seen her in with Elliot at Eric's funeral.

"Where did you get this?" I asked.

"I wanted to come home so I left the hotel. It was in the mail when I got here, addressed to Eric."

Seeing the envelope on the table I picked it up. There, in Eric's familiar handwriting, was Eric's name and address.

"He sent it to himself," I said. "He must have been trying to hide it, it wasn't with the others."

"Others?" queried Adele.

"Yes, the investigator that Elliot hired and I have been looking into whether there was anyone else that could have a reason to kill Eric. We found the apartment where all of this was filmed. Miranda Powell wasn't the only one."

"I never believed I was."

My blood chilled as I looked towards the doorway to

see Miranda Powell standing there, a gun in her hand pointed directly at Adele and me.

"Miranda," Adele said. "What are you doing? You're my friend. We've been friends since we were in high school."

"Then maybe you should have kept your hooks out of my husband," sneered Miranda.

I cringed, the fact she knew about Adele and Elliot did not bode well. Glancing at Adele, I saw a look of shame.

"I'm sorry. I am so, so sorry," Adele said, the tears rolling down her face.

"It was fine when Andrew was alive." Miranda went on as if ignoring Adele. "But then he died and you just fell apart. This whole pathetic need to be taken care of by a man. I was always there for him for years but he wanted the needy little girl who never stood on her own two feet."

Terrified as I was at that moment, I could understand why she was annoyed. Adele was no help as she sat blubbering in the chair and I fought the temptation to sigh in frustration. Even when our lives were on the line, Adele was incapable of stepping up and dealing with the situation. Taking a step forward, I regretted it immediately when the gun swung in my direction. The wound in my side started burning. My mouth went dry as I remembered the way it felt to have a bullet slice into you.

"Miranda, please think about what you are doing. You don't want to kill us. You're a doctor, you save people."

Miranda smiled. "You'd think so wouldn't you? I honestly thought I'd find it harder to kill, but Eric just made it so easy. I slept with him to get back at Adele. I could see that Elliot was slipping away from me. That he was falling in love with Adele and there was nothing I could do about it. I hated her so much and I wanted to hurt her. Eric started flirting with me, like he does with everyone, and I thought why not. Why shouldn't I take her husband the way she was taking mine? I slept with him once and thought that would be the end of it. Then he comes back to me and shows me the video. He told me that if I didn't pay him he would make sure that both Adele and Elliot knew what we did. He said he'd show them the video. I couldn't let him do that. I couldn't let that piece of garbage ruin my life."

"What did you do?" I asked, though by this point I was more interested in what our chances were of getting out of this alive.

"I swapped Adele's sleeping pills. Gave her a lot stronger version of what she normally has so that she would sleep through anything. Elliot had keys to the house so that night I let myself in, shot Eric and then moved Adele from her room into his. Made it look like she had never slept in her own bed."

"Hospital corners," I said, remembering Adele's perfectly made bed on the morning of the murder. "You were a nurse before you became a doctor weren't you."

"Very smart," said Miranda. "It's a pity you're so smart, but I was going to use that. I heard from Adele about the other murder case you were involved in. I thought it would be perfect if you found the gun, but I didn't get it in the safe until after you had been back to the house the first time. I kept trying to get you to go back and find the gun, but the police found it instead, which worked out so much better. Especially since I'd wiped it over her hands after killing Eric so they'd find gun residue on her. I couldn't think of anything more perfect than her being sent to jail for his murder. Unfortunately plans need to change, and I'm nothing if not adaptable."

"What are you going to do?" I asked, not wanting the answer to that particular question.

"There is going to be an unfortunate fire in the house, in fact it has already started," she said, and it was then that I could smell the smoke.

"A candle burning in Adele's bedroom has overturned on her bedding. It will take a little bit of time but this house will burn. It is far enough away from the neighbors that it shouldn't be reported until it's too late."

"You expect us to wait while we burn to death," I said incredulously.

"No," Miranda said as the gun that had been wavering between me and Adele suddenly straightened in my direction. "I will shoot you first, then Adele and leave the gun here. They'll think it was a murder and suicide. Everyone knows you've been helping that investigator look into Eric's death. You got all the evidence against Adele and she snapped and killed you. Realizing that she couldn't get away with your murder she killed herself. The overturned candle and resultant fire blurs the evidence, but it will be enough that no more questions will be asked.

Adele started whimpering and hearing the clinical explanation regarding my impending death, almost made me want to join her.

"What are you waiting for?" I asked.

"Just letting the fire gain some momentum. I have a plan, wouldn't want to start the ball rolling too early considering I'm going to be the one to report the fire."

"You're reporting the fire," I repeated, trying desperately to understand what was happening.

"Of course," Miranda said brightly. "I turned up to help Adele, like I always do, only to find the place engulfed in flames. I tried to get you out but I couldn't."

The smoke started to fill the room and Miranda pointed the gun at me.

"Looks like it's time to finish this," she said calmly. "Goodbye, Trudie. I'm sorry you got caught in the middle of this unfortunate situation."

I closed my eyes, not willing to see the bullet that was going to end my life, when I heard a smash and thud instead of the bang I was expecting. Opening my eyes, I saw Miranda slumped on the floor with Ruby standing over her, holding a horrible wood sculpture that Adele owned in her hands.

Rushing over, I kicked the gun away. Ruby looked at

Miranda, at the sculpture, and then at me.

"She was the one who killed Eric wasn't she?"

"Yes," I said as I pried the sculpture out of her hands before she decided to brain Miranda again. She looked dazed.

"Ruby, I need you to focus. We need to get out of here. There's a fire and I don't think we can put it out. Can you get Adele outside? At that moment I heard a crashing sound as the ceiling started to strain and I could see flames coming through the vents.

Heading towards Adele, Ruby turned. "What about her?" she asked, indicating the unconscious body on the ground.

Cursing the part of me that couldn't leave the woman who had tried to kill us, I grabbed hold of Miranda's limp body. I pushed Ruby towards Adele and the door. Once we were outside I saw the house being engulfed in flames. Ruby, Adele and I fell to the ground. Hearing sirens heading up the driveway I looked at Ruby.

"I called the police when I got here and saw her with the gun through the window," she said.

I grabbed her hand. "Thank you," I said gratefully, completely aware that Ruby had saved our lives.

Hearing Miranda moan, my eyes narrowed as she lifted her head up.

"Don't even think of trying to get away," I said as a squad car pulled up and two officers jumped out. As they approached us with guns drawn one yelled out.

"We got word of a gunman."

"It was her," Adele screeched, pointing at Miranda, and promptly fainted.

Chapter Twenty-Six

While the fire was brought under control Ruby and I sat at the back of an ambulance with blankets around our shoulders.

"Why did you come here?" I asked her. "I never thought I would see you anywhere around Adele."

"I wanted to see if there was anything of Eric's that he left me," she said. "I know it sounds silly but I just want to keep as much of him with me as possible."

We watched as Elliot Powell pulled up in his car, jumped out, completely ignored his wife sitting in the back of a squad car, and raced over to Adele's side as she lay on a stretcher in the back of an ambulance. Seeing the devastation on Miranda's face, I could almost feel sorry for her.

"I don't think you want any part of the Eric that lived in that house," I said slowly. "I think that you should hold onto the Eric that you had in your life, because nothing good came out of this place."

Ruby nodded. "I know people think I'm an idiot for staying with him and I probably was. Some people don't have the strength to walk away when a situation is not going to be good for them. I hope next time I'm stronger."

I nodded and then smiled as I saw Crystal pull up and get out of her car. Coming towards us I could see the concern written all over her face.

"I'm fine," I said, before she could open her mouth. She nodded and when I stood she wrapped her arms around my middle.

"You have to stop doing this to me," she said, and I could hear the unshed tears in her husky voice.

"I'm sorry," I said and squeezed her back.

I looked over her head to see Griffin had turned up

and was standing looking at us with concern in his eyes. I squeezed Crystal's shoulder.

"Can you give me a minute and then we can go home?" I asked.

She nodded and sniffed indelicately. Taking the blanket off, I walked over to Griffin.

"Are you okay?" he asked hesitantly.

"A tiny amount of smoke inhalation and a bit of a panic attack at having a gun pointed in my general direction again, but nothing major," I said lightly.

Griffin grimaced tightly. "You really need to find a safer job."

"Says the cop in one of the toughest cities in the country," I said, noting the irony. "Adele didn't kill Eric," I said.

"Yes, we've got your statements and Miranda just started confessing to anyone in hearing distance."

I looked over to see Ramos raptly listening to Miranda who was talking as animatedly as someone who was handcuffed could.

"Look," Griffin said. "I'm sorry I used you to get information regarding the case, but you need to understand it's my job. Being a cop is who I am. I can't let my personal life get in the way of that."

"I understand," I said. "And I admire your dedication to your job."

He smiled and stepped forward only to pull up short when I stepped back.

"And I'm sorry but what was between us will not work for me. I'm not cut out to take second place to your job."

I turned around and headed towards Crystal, fighting myself the whole way. I wanted so much to throw myself into his arms, but I could not have a relationship with him knowing that I came in second place to his job. Ruby was right. Sometimes you just needed to walk away.

About The Author

Leonie Gant started her writing career at the age of ten when she stuffed notes in her pencil case full of ideas for mysteries that Nancy Drew and the Hardy Boys should really have been solving. After years of watching mysteries play out in her head, she decided that writing them down was the best way to deal with them.

In her life away from writing, she is a voracious reader with not nearly enough time to make her way through all the books that she wants to read. She enjoys bushwalking, sewing and chocolate, possibly not in that order. She also believes in the value of trying new things, walking in the rain and enjoying every moment.

To find out more about Leonie Gant and her books
www.leoniegant.com

Discover other titles by Leonie Gant
Not Famous in Hollywood
Not Talented in Hollywood
Not Wanted in Hollywood
Not Suspicious in Hollywood
Not Forgotten in Hollywood

www.ingramcontent.com/pod-product-compliance
Lightning Source LLC
Chambersburg PA
CBHW021107130626
46554CB00002B/570